CLASSIC FOLK TALES

80 TRADITIONAL STORIES FROM AROUND THE WORLD

RETOLD BY NICOLA BAXTER
ILLUSTRATED BY ROGER LANGTON

ARMADILLO

Publisher: Joanna Lorenz
Compiled by: Nicola Baxter
Research: Gordon Alexander Smith
Designer: Amanda Hawkes
Production Designer: Amy Barton
Production Controller: Don Campaniello

A CIP catalogue record for this book is available
from the British Library.

PUBLISHER'S NOTE
The author and publishers have made every
effort to ensure that this book is safe for its
intended use, and cannot accept any legal
responsibility or liability for any harm or injury
arising from misuse.

This edition is published by Armadillo,
an imprint of Anness Publishing Ltd,
Blaby Road, Wigston, Leicestershire
LE18 4SE; info@anness.com

www.annesspublishing.com

If you like the images in this book and would
like to investigate using them for publishing,
promotions or advertising, please visit our
website www.practicalpictures.com for more
information.

© Anness Publishing Ltd 2012

Manufacturer: Anness Publishing Ltd,
Blaby Road, Wigston, Leicestershire
LE18 4SE, England
For Product Tracking go to:
www.annesspublishing.com/tracking
Batch: 5898-20425-1127

CONTENTS

THE AMERICAS

THE ANIMALS WHO COULD TALK

 Many, many years ago, in the Distant Time, humans and animals lived more closely together.

In fact, they could even talk to each other, for in the cold, dark lands, animals wore hoods, as humans still do today. When the animals drew back their hoods, they had human faces underneath and could laugh and talk and sing just as we can.

Once there were two brothers who spent many months journeying. Wherever they went, little people invited them into their homes and showed them great kindness. But strangely enough, each time the boys left, their hosts told them to go a certain distance before they turned and looked back.

You know, it was the strangest thing, but once when they looked back, the boys could see no house at all, but a beaver's lodge across a river, with two beavers swimming outside.

Another time, they saw swirling murky water, and a seal family sliding through the waves.

One brother stayed for a while in a large house where several small human couples and their families were also staying. Hearing that the head of the household had not long to live, the brother agreed to marry his host's only daughter.

At once, all the couples in the house pulled up their hoods and turned into different kinds of birds. They flew around the happy couple, each singing a different song.

But when the boy looked at his bride, she was not a bird at all, but a full-sized human person. Together, the boy and his bride went out into the world, to live among the animals they knew and loved so well.

THE RAVEN: BRINGER OF LIGHT

 Long ago, a chief called his people together and said, "As you know, only one village in our land has light. I will give the hand of my elder daughter to whoever can bring that light back to us."

Many young men set off with high hopes, but if they found the light, no one knows, for they never returned.

At last, the Raven spoke up. "I will bring you light!" he cawed. Everyone laughed.

The Raven flew off into the darkness. Day after day, he flew, until at last he saw a faint light in the distance. As he flew nearer, the light grew brighter and brighter, until it was so strong he could hardly see.

In the middle of the Village of Light was a spring. The Raven watched and waited. When the chief's daughter came to drink, he changed himself into a tiny feather that floated on the surface. The girl swallowed him.

Nine months later, the chief's daughter gave birth to a son – a raven! Everyone loved him and gave him everything he wanted. The little Raven soon realized that the light must be hidden in one of three caskets on a high shelf in the chief's home.

One night, when the chief was asleep, the Raven opened the boxes. In the first was night. In the second were the moon and the stars. The third contained the precious light.

Taking the second and third caskets in his mouth, the Raven flew off back to his old village. Everyone crowded around.

"I have brought you light," said the Raven, and he showed them the moon and the stars.

The people were overjoyed. As he had promised, the chief gave the Raven his elder daughter in marriage.

But the next day, the Raven said, "What if I gave you an even greater light?" And he opened the third casket, with the sun inside.

What could the chief give the Raven? His younger daughter, of course! The Raven and his wives lived happily ever after by the light of the sun and the moon and the stars.

MOTHER SWAN AND HER BEAUTIFUL DAUGHTERS

Mother Swan raised her daughters by herself. When they were ready to be married, she said to the elder two, Round Stone and Long Legs, "Bake some marriage bread and take it to the land of the Eagle people. There you will find Great Mother Earthquake. Her son, Scar Face, will make you both a fine husband. But do not stop on the way."

The girls made their marriage bread and set off, but on the way they met a man of the Owl people. He tricked the girls and stole their marriage bread. Sadly, they returned home to Mother Swan.

"Round Stone, you must stay at home now," said the old woman. "Long Legs, you must bake more marriage bread and this time take your younger sister, Shaking Leaf. And remember, do not stop on the way."

Round Stone and Shaking Leaf did as they were told, but once again the Owl man met them.

"Great Mother Earthquake lives over there," he said, pointing to his own lodge. As the girls approached, the Owl man hurried along and went in by another entrance.

Inside the lodge, it was very dark. The girls thought that the Owl man was Scar Face and his wife was Great Mother Earthquake. Luckily, just at that moment, a messenger came from the Eagle people, asking the Owl man to come. He did not like to upset Great Mother Earthquake, so he hurried away. Round Stone and Shaking Leaf realized their mistake and hurried after him.

At Great Mother Earthquake's lodge, the girls were kindly received. Scar Face was only too happy to take them as his wives. And Great Mother Earthquake sent for Mother Swan and her remaining daughter to come and live with the Eagle people, where they would have a warm fire and good food always.

BLACK BART: THE POET DESPERADO

 "How glad I am we are almost there!" sighed a lady in a dark green cape. Riding on the dusty, rattling Wells Fargo stagecoach was not at all comfortable. Now San Francisco was only an hour away. Everyone felt their spirits rise.

But a moment later, a strange figure leapt from the bushes beside the road. A man in a pale duster coat, with a flour sack over his head and a derby hat perched on top of that, was pointing a shotgun at the terrified driver.

"Throw down the box!" cried a deep voice.

He meant the treasure box, in which the Wells Fargo stage carried gold and money to its bank in the city.

The driver did as he was told at once.

The robber appeared to have no interest in the passengers at all, but the lady in the cape lost her head.

"Take my purse!" she shrieked, flinging it through the window.

But the stranger picked up the purse and returned it to her with a bow.

"Thank you, ma'am, but I don't need your money. I only want Wells Fargo's."

In minutes, the robber had disappeared, but he left something else for the surprised passengers. In place of the contents of the treasure box was a poem, and the signature below it was a joke in itself. It read: "The Po8".

Black Bart, as the robber came to be known, struck twenty-seven times before he finally met his match. He fled, but he dropped a handkerchief as he ran. The laundry mark told the detectives all they needed to know. Black Bart was none other than a respectable mining engineer called Charles Bolton.

Black Bart's career was over, but Charles Bolton survived his prison term and emerged with a smile still on his face. He vowed that there would be no more crime – and no more poems – in his extraordinary life. As far as anyone knows, there never were.

THE MYSTERY OF ROANOKE

When Europeans began to settle in what they called the New World, there were, of course, already people living there. They were the first Americans, but the Europeans called them Indians, mainly because in the early days they were very confused about where America was!

The British adventurer Sir Walter Ralegh was one of those who thought he might be able to make his fortune by sending goods and people to form a settlement on the East Coast of America. It wasn't an easy business raising funds to do this, but at last an expedition was ready to set sail. Three ships left London in April 1587.

There were problems right from the start, and it was a much smaller band of people than originally planned who eventually arrived off the coast of what we now call Virginia. They made a settlement on an island far up an estuary. It was called Roanoke.

The settlers relied very heavily on having the help and goodwill of the people they called Indians. Things were not easy, but everyone worked hard. There were even babies born in the new settlement.

Now Sir Walter Ralegh knew that new settlements needed a lot of help and support. He fully intended to send ships with more supplies within a few months. Unfortunately, a war with the Spanish started up, which rather took his mind off the settlers. It was almost three years before another ship went in support of the colony.

When the ship's commander reached Roanoke, he found no settlers, and no sure sign of what had happened to them.

It was not until 1701, over a hundred years later, that a surveyor, working in the area, came across a band of native people with pale skin and light brown hair. Were they the descendants of the settlers, who had married the local Indians? It seemed that it might indeed be so.

12

LAPIN AND THE TAR BABY

Now Rabbit (but in this part of the world he is called Lapin) loved vegetables, and he wasn't too choosy about who they belonged to when his big front teeth went chomping and chewing.

Mr. Bouki knew very well that Lapin came into his garden each night and stole all the best, ripest and freshest vegetables. He thought about the matter for a few days and came up with a plan.

The next night, when Lapin came into the garden, he found a little girl sitting right in the middle of the vegetable patch. He didn't realize, in the moonlight, that she was made of straw and tar.

"Move over," said Lapin. "I'm feeling hungry and I see some fine carrots just behind you."

But the little girl didn't move. Lapin pushed her – hard – with his paw, and the paw stuck fast. In frustration, Lapin pushed with his other paw, and it got stuck as well. Then Lapin kicked with both his big feet, and they got well and truly stuck, too.

In the morning, Mr. Bouki found Lapin and pulled him off the tar baby. "Now, what shall I do with *you*?" he wondered.

Lapin clasped his paws together and cried, "Oh, Mr. Bouki, skin me and fry me or boil me in a basin, but *please* don't throw me in the briar patch."

"Frying sounds good," said Mr. Bouki.

"Oh, thank you, thank you," cried Lapin. "As long as it isn't the briar patch."

"Or I certainly could boil you," said Mr. Bouki thoughtfully.

"That's fine!" cried Lapin. "Anything but the briar patch!"

Then Mr. Bouki made up his mind. He threw Lapin as hard as he could right into the middle of the briar patch.

Then a cheeky face popped up. "Nothing I like better than a briar patch, Mr. Bouki. Thank you very much!" laughed Lapin.

BORREGUITA OUTWITS COYOTE

There was once a little lamb called Borreguita. To Coyote, she looked like a plump and perfect morsel for his supper. But when he jumped out in front of Borreguita as she sat peacefully watching the sunset, she did not seem afraid.

"Don't be silly, Coyote," she said. "A big, brave animal like you needs a larger supper than me. Under this wool I'm terribly small and skinny. Why don't you wait until I grow?"

Coyote didn't want to wait, but he didn't want to look silly either. He sat down nearby and watched with Borreguita as the sun went down and the big round moon came up.

Pretty soon, Coyote didn't care *how* small Borreguita was. He was really hungry.

The lamb saw him licking his lips. "Hey, Coyote!" she called. "Look in this pool! A perfect supper for you!"

"What is it?" asked Coyote, peering in.

"It's a huge cheese, silly!" (that word again…) laughed the lamb. "It's sitting at the bottom of this pool keeping cool. It will be absolutely delicious!"

So Coyote jumped right into the pool – and the reflection of the moon disappeared!

When Coyote climbed out of the water, Borreguita was nowhere to be seen. It was a couple of days before Coyote caught up with her. Borreguita had seen him coming. She was sitting with her back to the hillside with an expression of concentration on her face.

"Don't interrupt me, Coyote," she said. "The mountain is about to fall on top of us and I'm … just … managing to hold it up."

"Never mind that," said Coyote. "You're going to be my lunch!"

"Well that would be silly, wouldn't it?" said Borreguita. "Eat me, and the mountain will fall down on top of you."

"All right," said Coyote. "I'll hold up the mountain. Then it won't matter if I eat you."

"OK," said Borreguita. As soon as Coyote was in position, she skipped away.

As for Coyote, maybe he's still holding up that mountain. Or maybe not…

ROSAMADA AND THE PRINCE OF DARKNESS

Rosamada was a beautiful young woman but she was also very proud. None of the young men who came to court her were good enough for her. She declared that she would only marry a real prince.

But year after year passed, and no prince came looking for Rosamada. Her beauty began to fade, and people said she would never get married now.

Then, one day, a handsome young man came to town. No one knew where he came from, but there was a swagger to his walk and a glint in his eye that was bewitching.

Rosamada had to work hard to make the young man notice her, but at last he did. To her great delight, he asked for her hand in marriage. Her father, having given up all hope of marrying his daughter, agreed.

The wedding was magnificent, even if the bride's beauty had become a little hard and brittle, and the bridegroom's gaze had a strange light in it.

After the ceremony, the bridegroom took Rosamada to a mysterious castle in the far mountains. He smiled – and his teeth seemed very sharp and long. He swept off his hat – and his hair seemed to curl into two little horns. He removed his gloves – and his nails looked almost like claws. But when he took off his boots, Rosamada was sure. He did not have feet but cloven hoofs. She had married a prince indeed – the prince of darkness. It was the devil himself who stood before her.

"Not so proud now, Rosamada," he mocked her, as his eyes glittered in the lamplight. Then, in a flash of fire, the castle and the mountains disappeared.

It is said that Rosamada was found in the forest, unconscious on the ground. She was carried back to her father's house, but it was no use. Within six months the proud princess was married to her grave.

ANANSI AND THE BUNCH OF PLANTAINS

Anansi the spider never did any work, but somehow he managed to do pretty well all the same.

One day, Anansi's wife said to him, "We have nothing in the house to eat and the children are hungry. Go out and find us something!"

Anansi strolled down the road until he found Rat, who was carrying a large bunch of plantains, which are like bananas.

"These are the very last from my field," said Rat. "They'll have to last us a while."

Then Anansi put on a very sad face and told Rat that his children had nothing to eat at all that night.

Anansi sounded so pitiful that Rat broke off four plantains and handed them to the spider. But Anansi still looked sad.

"The thing is, Rat," he said, "there are five of us and only four plantains."

But Rat felt this was going too far. He walked quickly on as if he had not heard.

Anansi took the plantains home and gave them to his wife and three children, who began to eat hungrily. But one of the children noticed that Anansi was not eating.

"Aren't you hungry, Papa?" he asked.

"Yes, I'm hungry. I'm very, very hungry," replied Anansi, "but there were only four plantains and there are five of us. It's best if you take them. I'll be all right … I expect."

"No, no! That's not fair!" cried the youngest child, and he broke off half his plantain and gave it to his father.

Then the other two children and Anansi's wife felt guilty too. They did the same thing.

Anansi would have thanked them … but he had his mouth full.

You may have noticed that while everyone else got half a banana each, Anansi ended up with two all to himself. It's funny the way that spider always seems to get the best end of a deal…

ANANSI TRIES TO GAIN WISDOM

Anansi was always looking for ways to better himself, and one day he thought of a plan to gain wisdom. He knew that he was clever, but he realized that he wasn't very wise.

Anansi took a big hollowed-out gourd and set off around the village. He stopped in front of each house he came to and called out to the inhabitants, "Could you spare a poor spider a little bit of wisdom?"

This made most of the animals smile. They thought it wasn't a bad idea for Anansi to be a bit wiser, so they dropped a little something into his gourd.

By the time Anansi had been all round the village, his gourd was full to overflowing.

"I'm certainly the wisest person I know, now," said Anansi, "but where am I going to keep all this? I wouldn't want it to fall into the wrong hands."

Anansi decided to store his wisdom at the top of a tall tree, so he picked a particularly handsome palm, tied the gourd in front of him, and started to try to climb the tree.

It was hopeless. With the gourd in front of him, Anansi's legs couldn't even reach the tree trunk.

"What are you doing, Papa?" asked Anansi's son, who happened to be passing.

When Anansi explained, the boy grinned. "Wouldn't you get on better if you tied the gourd to your back instead of your front?"

It was a good plan. In no time, Anansi had reached the top of the tree, but as he sat there, he became thoughtful.

"I've got all this wisdom," he said to himself, "but even my son is sometimes wiser than me." Then he threw the wisdom in the gourd out across the land below, for it didn't seem very useful after all.

And that is how wisdom came to be spread all over the world.

THE CLEVER GULL MOTHER

 On the shores of Lake Titicaca there lived a gull. She made herself a nest among the stones on the lake shore and settled down to raise a family.

In time, she laid three eggs, and in more time still, the eggs hatched out into three fluffy chicks. They squawked a lot and they were always hungry. The mother gull had to fly off to catch fish for them over and over again, until she was exhausted.

One day, when the gull was away fishing, a cunning fox crept up to the nest. There was nothing he liked more than baby gulls for his supper. Quick as a flash, he popped the chicks into his supper sack and hurried away.

The mother gull returned just in time to hear her babies squawking. She followed, high overhead, to see where the fox went. Meanwhile, the gulls squawked and pecked at the fox through the sack, until his back and shoulders were sore all over.

Pretty soon, the fox was so tired of tramping in the hot sun with a heavy sack of awkward birds that he sat down under a thorn bush. He laid a stone over the opening of the sack and went to sleep.

Now the mother bird saw her chance. She swooped down and pushed the stone from the sack. Then the chicks helped her to fill the sack with thorn branches, before they pushed the stone back into position. At last, one at a time, she carried the chicks back to the lake, where she made a new nest, well away from the first one.

When the fox woke up, he set off once more. The thorns stabbed into him just as the chicks' beaks had done, so he didn't suspect a thing … until he sat down to eat his supper.

All that old fox got was a sore paw to add to his sore back and shoulders. So the fox went hungry to bed. And the mother gull? Well, she didn't get to bed at all – she was too busy fishing for her hungry children!

THE BIRDS AND THE MONSTER

Once there was a boy who lived in the rainforest. He liked nothing better than taking his bow and arrow and setting off to see what he could shoot. All the birds of the forest were frightened of him. He had killed so many of their friends and relatives. When the boy was about, the birds fell silent, and the forest was a sad place.

One day, the boy walked further into the forest than he had ever done before. He paddled his canoe down the winding Amazon River, then gathered his bow and arrow and walked softly along the river bank.

Tall trees towered overhead, but near the river there were smaller bushes, full of flowers. The boy walked until he came to a place where the birds were still singing.

But just as the boy was creeping close to a family of parrots, chattering on a branch, he heard a horrible sound. It was a kind of whistling. All at once, the boy who had never felt frightened in his life found that his knees were trembling. There was something about that sound that was truly terrifying.

Suddenly, the boy felt a hot breath on his neck. Turning, he saw a ghastly monster, with huge claws, a hairy body, a thrashing tail, and a hole in his head that made the whistling sound. The boy was so scared, he could not move. "Help!" he cried.

"Why should we help you?" squawked the parrots, who had flown up to a higher branch. "We've heard of you. All you do is shoot us."

"If you help me, I promise I will never shoot another bird!" cried the boy, staring into the fierce eyes of the monster.

Then the birds and all their brightly feathered friends flew up into the air and swooped on the monster, pecking and clawing at him until he ran away.

The boy kept his promise, and the rainforest is full of the sound of singing, laughing, chattering birds to this day.

THE ARMADILLO AND THE FOX

Foxes are clever creatures, but even they are sometimes not clever enough. One day, Fox was walking through the world when he saw Armadillo.

"What are you doing, Armadillo?" asked Fox, as Armadillo put brushwood in long piles.

"I'm making a fence," said Armadillo, "so that all and sundry can't walk over here."

"And why would you worry about that?" asked Fox, intrigued.

"Because I'm going to plant some crops," said Armadillo.

Now Fox was very interested indeed. "Well, I can't see any problem there," he said. "It would be only fair, though, to share with your friends. What if you gave me everything that grows above ground and kept for yourself everything that grows below ground?"

Armadillo agreed … with a smile. When Fox came back at the end of the season, he was not best pleased to find that Armadillo had planted potatoes! Under the ground were tasty tubers – enough to feed a whole armadillo family. Above the ground were leaves – not good for even a single sorry fox to eat.

"I can see I have made a mistake," said Fox. "What I should have said was: you can have everything above the ground, and I will take everything that grows below the ground."

"Yes, that would be better," said old Armadillo with a broad smile.

At the end of the following season, Fox came along, licking his lips.

"I've just finished my harvest," cried Armadillo. "Look how many beautiful heads of corn I have picked. Oh, and the roots for you are over there." He pointed to a small, sorry-looking pile.

Then Fox slunk away to plan his revenge. And Armadillo set about making a fabulous feast for his family. He was still smiling…

THE WITCH
OF WINTER

 For people who live in the high mountains, winter can be a terrible time. In the Andes, there is a story that, at the same time every year, a horrible witch wakes from her summer sleep and touches the land with her crooked fingers to bring a deadly cold. The earth becomes hard as iron. The rocks are frosted with snow. And the lakes freeze over.

One year, a boy and his sister went further into the mountains than they should, dazzled by the glittering and glimmering of light on the snow. At last, the little girl was too tired to go on, but she was far from home. She lay down near a rock and gradually became colder and colder, until she could no longer move. The witch had her firmly in her icy grip.

"Only fire defeats the frost!" cried a condor sailing overhead.

When he heard that, the boy ran off to get help. At last, he found a little hut, with a man inside crouching over the glowing embers of a small fire.

"Please let me borrow some fire to save my sister!" cried the boy.

With a smile, the man held a branch in the embers until it caught fire. "Run, boy, but take care!" he said.

But in his hurry, the boy splashed too quickly through a river he had to cross, and the water put the flames out. He ran all the way back to the hut. Once again, the man gave him a flaming branch.

This time, the boy was very careful, but as he crossed a ravine, he dropped the branch, and watched the flames fizzle out in the snow.

For the last time, the boy ran back to the hut. It was growing dark, and he knew that his sister could not have long to live.

As night fell, the boy reached the little girl. He set fire to some nearby moss and twigs, and she woke from her sleep of icy death and held out her arms.

With a cackle like cracking ice, the witch of winter, defeated again, slowly left the land.

EUROPE

TURN AGAIN, WHITTINGTON!

There was once a poor boy called Dick Whittington who set off to London to make his fortune. When he arrived, he could not believe the hustle and bustle all around him. But there were no streets paved with gold as he had heard.

At last he found a job in the kitchen of a wealthy man, Mr. Fitzwarren. Dick had a little room at the top of the house. But the work was hard, and at night his room was so over-run with rats and mice that he couldn't sleep.

Resourceful Dick went out and bought a cat. At once, things improved. He could sleep at night, and the cat was a real friend.

Now Mr. Fitzwarren was a merchant, sending trading ships overseas. One day he gathered his servants and told them that if they wanted to make a little money by trading themselves, they could send goods on the ship now ready to depart. All the servants did so, but Dick didn't own anything to sell. Suddenly, he had an idea. He sent the only possession he had to the ship. It was his cat!

Without the cat, Dick was lonely and once more troubled by rats and mice at night. Sadly, he decided that success in London had only been a dream. He set out for home.

But as Dick reached the outskirts of the city, he heard the bells of Bow Church ring out. *Ding dong! Turn again, Whittington, Lord Mayor of London!* their deep voices seemed to say. Dick couldn't believe it, but something made him retrace his steps all the same.

Meanwhile, Dick's cat had killed all the mice and rats on the ship, much to the crew's delight. Then, in a foreign country where cats were not known, he was sold for a huge sum to a rich king who also had a problem with little scuttling creatures.

When the ship came home, Dick became a wealthy man. He married Mr. Fitzwarren's daughter and became a successful merchant. And yes, one day, he did indeed become Lord Mayor of London.

FAITHFUL GREYFRIARS BOBBY

 John Gray, known to his friends as Jock, was buried in Greyfriars Churchyard in 1858. As far as we know, there was nothing remarkable about the funeral except that one of the chief mourners was a dog! Jock's little Skye terrier Bobby was devastated by his master's death. From that day, he spent each night guarding the grave, not moving from his post in even the most dreadful winter weather.

Well, there are rules about these things, and James Brown, who looked after the burial ground, tried hard to move the dog away. There was, after all, a sign on the gate saying that dogs were not permitted inside.

But Bobby would not be moved. He always found a way back to the grave of his greatest friend. After a while, James Brown felt sorry for the dog. He brought him some food and, in recognition of his faithful love for his master, allowed him to stay.

Year after year, Bobby sat on Jock's grave. In fact, fourteen long years passed before, on a cold January day in 1872, the little dog died. Perhaps he was able to greet his master again at last.

Although Greyfriars Bobby, as he had come to be known, was gone, his memory lived on. Many people felt that such devotion should be marked in some way. One wealthy woman, Baroness Burdett Coutts, did more than think about it. She paid for a fountain to be erected, with a statue of the little dog on top, which was unveiled in November 1873.

Today, the story of Greyfriars Bobby is known all over the world, and his statue never lacks visitors.

THE GOOD LUCK ELVES

Rowli Pugh was married to a woman called Catti Jones. Although they had a cottage and a little land, nothing ever seemed to go right for them. The roof leaked. The cattle grew thin. Catti herself became ill and was not able to look after Rowli or the home. Things got so bad that Rowli decided he must sell up and seek his fortune elsewhere.

One morning, as Rowli sat by his run-down cottage, planning how to leave, he saw to his surprise that a little elf was standing in front of him.

"Don't worry," said the elf. "Just ask your wife to leave a lighted candle in the hearth tonight when you go to bed."

It sounded odd, but Rowli had nothing to lose. He told Catti to leave a candle alight.

The next morning, the couple were delighted to find that the cottage was clean and the furniture polished. There was fresh water drawn from the well and new bread in the oven. Even Rowli's torn and dirty clothes had been washed and mended.

And so it went on. Each night, Catti left a lighted candle in the hearth. In the morning, a whole night's work had been done.

It wasn't long before Rowli and Catti began to feel like different people. Rowli went about his land with new energy and enthusiasm. Catti took a pride in doing her part in keeping the family happy and prosperous. There was no more talk of selling up and moving on.

One night, many years later, Catti could live with her curiosity no longer. She got up while Rowli slept and peeped through the door. Lots of little elves were hard at work in the next room. Catti laughed so hard that the elves heard her. They were gone in an instant and never returned, but it didn't matter. The family's bad luck never returned either.

THE FIELD OF GOLD

On a sunny day at harvest time, a lad was walking along when he heard a little tapping sound. He peered into the hedge and saw a tiny man in a leather apron, mending a little shoe.

"Well, well, well," said the young man to himself. "I truly never expected to meet a leprechaun. Now that I have, I must not let this chance slip away. Everyone knows that leprechauns keep a pot of gold hidden nearby. All I have to do is to find it and I am made for life."

The lad greeted the leprechaun politely and enquired after his health, but after a few minutes of idle chit-chat, the boy became impatient. He grabbed the leprechaun and demanded to be taken to the gold.

"All right, all right!" cried the little man. "It is near here. I'll show you."

The strange pair set off over the fields, with the boy being careful never to take his eyes off his little guide. At last they came to a field of golden ragwort.

The leprechaun pointed to a large plant.

"The gold is under here," he said. "All you have to do is to dig down and find it."

Now the lad did not have a spade or shovel with him but he was not stupid. He pulled off his red neckerchief and tied it to the plant so that he would recognize it again.

"Promise me," he said to the leprechaun, "that you will not untie that scarf."

The little man promised faithfully.

Then the lad dropped the leprechaun and ran home as fast as he could to fetch a spade. He was back at the side of the field within five minutes. But what a sight met his eyes! Every single ragwort plant in the whole field – and there were hundreds – had a red neckerchief tied around it.

Slowly, the boy walked home with his spade, sadder and wiser. He didn't have the gold. He didn't have the leprechaun. And now, he didn't even have his neckerchief!

THE FAIRY MOUSE

 There was once a queen and her baby daughter who were imprisoned by an evil king. Each day, they were brought only a morsel of black bread and three peas each to eat.

The queen had been raised in comfort, but she had a kind heart. When a little mouse crept out of the wall and rubbed its tiny tummy to show how hungry it was, she gave it one of her peas to eat. At once, a wonderful meal appeared on the table.

Day after day, the same thing happened. The queen no longer feared that she and her daughter would starve, but she was very worried about the future of her child. One day, the mouse brought in some wisps of straw.

"Oh," cried the queen, "if only I had more straw, I could weave a basket and lower my baby from the window. Then perhaps a kind passer-by would take her to safety and look after her for me."

After that, the little mouse brought in more and more straw, until the basket was almost finished. The queen looked out of the window to judge the height and saw below an old, old woman.

"Please," called the queen, "could you help me?" She explained about her baby.

"Certainly I can," replied the old woman, "but I need something in return. I love to eat a plump roast mouse, but there are none to be found hereabouts. Could you get me one?"

The queen shook her head. She wanted more than anything to save her child, but she could not kill a creature that had been so good to them both.

Suddenly, the little mouse appeared and before the queen's astonished eyes, it turned into a beautiful fairy!

"You have shown that you know the meaning of true friendship," said the fairy. "I will take you away to my magical castle, where you and your daughter can live happily ever after." And so she did.

BROTHERS FIGHT BROTHERS

In ancient times, there was a king called Numitor who ruled the city of Alba Longa. He had a beautiful daughter, Rhea Silvia.

Numitor's jealous brother Amulius seized the city and imprisoned its rightful king. He forced Rhea Silvia to dedicate her life to the gods, giving up the hope of marriage and a family of her own. But Mars, the god of war, had seen how beautiful Rhea Silvia was. He visited her one night in secret.

Nine months later, Rhea Silvia gave birth to twin boys and named them Romulus and Remus. But her wicked uncle, fearful that the boys would grow up and seek their revenge, threw the babies and their mother into the River Tiber.

Rhea Silvia drowned in the rushing waters, but the babies were washed ashore. They were found by a she-wolf, who heard their crying as she prowled along the

riverbank. Instead of eating them, she carried them home and raised them as her own, suckling them just as she did her own cubs.

One day, a shepherd named Faustulus found the little boys, who had grown into sturdy children. The shepherd had formerly worked for King Numitor and knew at once who the boys must be. He took them home and cared for them. When they were old enough, he told them who they truly were.

Romulus and Remus killed their great-uncle and freed their grandfather. Then, to mark their good fortune, they built a city on the banks of the Tiber, in the place where they had been found. Alas, the boys disagreed over who should rule the city. Romulus killed Remus and became the king. He called his city Rome. It is standing to this day.

THE OLD MAN AND THE FAITHFUL ANIMALS

Once there was an old man who had worked for many years in a mill. When he told his master that he could no longer do the heavy work required, the miller threw him out without a penny.

The old man went to say goodbye to the animals who lived at the mill. They had never shown him anything but kindness.

"Goodbye, old Horse. Goodbye, Ox. Goodbye, Cat and Dog and Rooster," he said.

The animals did not hesitate. They did not want to stay with the mean old miller and followed their friend out into the world.

The friends journeyed together until they came to a forest. By now they were all tired and hungry. Then, in a clearing, they found a beautiful house. Next to it was a barn full of hay, while all around lay a garden full of flourishing fruit and vegetables.

The friends waited and waited, but no one came. At last, the old man decided they should take advantage of all the house could offer.

After a satisfying meal, the horse went to sleep at one side of the barn, while the ox snored on the other side. The rooster dozed on the roof, and the dog slept by the front door of the house. Inside, the cat found a comfy place by the fire, and the old man sank into a soft bed upstairs.

In the middle of the night, the robber who owned the house came home. He crept up to his bedroom and heard the old man's snores. How loud they sounded in the still of the night! Fleeing downstairs, the robber trod on the cat's tail. With a screech, she flew up and scratched his face.

The robber rushed outside, only to fall over the dog, who growled and bit him. Then the ox butted him with his horns, and the horse delivered a well-aimed kick. As the robber ran from the clearing, the rooster landed on his head and made a dreadful noise.

The more the robber thought about it, the surer he was that demons had occupied his house. He vowed never to return. So the old man and the animals had their reward at last and lived happily ever after.

THE TRUE VALUE OF SALT

 Once there was a king with three beautiful daughters. One day, he called them together and said, "I want you all to think very carefully about what you choose for my birthday present. I will give my kingdom to the one who chooses the gift that is most essential to life."

On the king's birthday, the two eldest girls gave him costly but useful presents. Then the youngest princess brought her gift. It was a simple wooden container of salt.

The king was furious. "Don't you care about me at all?" he cried. He banished his youngest daughter from the palace.

Weeping, she wandered through the world until she met a woman who kept an inn. This woman gave the princess a home – and something much more valuable. She taught her how to cook. Soon the girl's cooking was famed throughout the land.

In time, the king's eldest daughter chose a husband. Wanting to do the best for his child, the king asked the famous cook to prepare the wedding banquet, not knowing who she really was.

Of course, the food was wonderful. The guests loved every delicious mouthful.

But when the king asked for his own best-loved dish to be brought to him, he threw down his knife in disgust.

"This meal is tasteless!" he cried. "Why, it has no salt in it at all!"

When the cook was summoned, she stood proud and still. "Once, Your Highness," she said, "you banished your own daughter for daring to suggest that salt is essential."

Then the king recognized his daughter and his own foolishness. Welcoming her with open arms, he vowed never to divide his family again.

THE BOY WHO SAVED A TOWN

The Netherlands and the surrounding nations are sometimes known as the Low Countries. That is because the land is flat and low-lying. Without protection, it would always be at the mercy of the sea, which could pour in and swallow it up at any moment. However, Dutch engineers have cleverly built a system of ditches and walled banks, called dykes, to channel water away from the fields.

Every Dutch child grows up knowing how important the dykes are and how disastrous it would be if the water broke through.

One day a boy of about eight was walking home along the top of a dyke when he heard a little trickling sound. Looking down, he saw that there was a tiny hole in the wall of the dyke, and water was escaping through it. Even as he watched, the force of the water made the hole a little bigger.

The boy looked all around, but there was not another person in sight. He knew that the water would soon become a torrent, and if the whole wall collapsed, all the land around would be flooded, including the nearby town.

Without hesitating, he kneeled down and put his finger in the hole.

Minutes passed. Hours passed. The boy's hand and arm began to ache, but he dare not let go. If only someone would come along!

When night fell, the boy knew that no one else would pass there before dawn. Cold and uncomfortable, he still did not move. The moon rose above him.

It was not until the next morning that a passing minister spotted the boy and released him from his task. Before long, the dyke was repaired and everyone was safe.

The boy went quietly home, but the minister made sure that everyone knew what had happened, and how even the smallest action can have a huge effect.

THE PIED PIPER OF HAMELIN

 Hundreds of years ago, the people of Hamelin had a problem. Rats! They were everywhere! They ate all the food and frightened the children. They were so big and fat that even the cats and dogs of the town were afraid of them.

The people protested to their Mayor, and he in turn offered a reward of a thousand guilders to anyone who could solve the problem. All sorts of people tried to win the reward, but no one succeeded.

Then, one day, along came a very strange-looking man. He was dressed in a long gown, old and ragged, that was half red and half yellow! His long cap had bells on it.

"I can solve your problem," he said, and he drew from his belt a long, thin pipe.

Well, when the piper began to play, every rat in the place came running out to hear the music. And as the piper walked along, the scurrying creatures all followed him. The odd man led them out of the town as far as the river. As he stepped onto a boat and pushed himself away from the quay, the rats all tried to follow. They fell one by one into the water, where they were all drowned.

Then, of course, the Pied Piper went to the Mayor for his reward. But the Mayor, reasoning that the rats could not come back from the dead, refused to pay it. "Quite right!" said the townspeople.

The Pied Piper smiled. Suddenly, he looked even stranger and more sinister. Picking up his pipe, he began to play one more time.

This time it was not rats that followed the piper but children. They could not help themselves. As he played, they had to follow.

The Pied Piper led them out of the town and into the hills, where they disappeared into a cave under the mountain.

Then the people of Hamelin were sorry they had tricked the piper, but it was too late. They never saw their children again.

THE STORY OF OLENTZERO

Long ago, in the Basque country of northern Spain, there was a beautiful fairy with long golden hair. She went around doing good to people, helped by some little elves in red trousers.

One day in the mountains, the little elves found a human baby, left all alone among the ferns. The kind fairy took the baby to a couple who lived nearby. They had no children of their own, so they were very happy to have the baby, whom the fairy called Olentzero.

Olentzero grew into a brave and kind man. His parents were very proud of him, but eventually they grew old and died. Then Olentzero was alone in the cottage in the mountains. As the years passed, his hair grew white and he could not work so hard. But Olentzero badly wanted to help people. One day, he decided to make some children's toys in his little workshop.

Olentzero enjoyed making the toys, but he knew what would be even better. Loading his donkey, he made the long journey through the mountains to the nearest town.

It was a day of happiness for everyone.

The children loved the toys, and Olentzero loved giving them away. From that day, Olentzero was a welcome sight in the town.

Then, one year, a terrible storm blew up as Olentzero arrived. Before his eyes, a house was struck by lightning and burst into flames. Brave Olentzero rushed into the flames to save the children inside. In doing so, he lost his own life.

As the children wept outside, everyone was astonished to see a bright light inside the ruined house. It was the fairy. She could not bear Olentzero's generous life and good heart to end, so she had come to do her magic.

From that day, in the middle of each winter, Olentzero and the fairy's little elves take toys to children who have no parents or grandparents to give them presents, and the kind, brave man's name lives on.

THE LOVERS AND THE LAKES

 Almost five hundred years ago, it is said, Portuguese sailors discovered a group of islands far out in the Atlantic Ocean. They were named the Azores. It was not long before it was realized how useful these could be as trading ports. The King of Portugal, delighted by his new territories, insisted on visiting them.

Now the king had a very beautiful daughter with the deepest blue eyes anyone had ever seen. Rather than leave her at home, where some unscrupulous nobleman might pay court to her, the king took the princess with him to the islands.

Once there, the king spent many days in discussions about the area's future. In the meantime, the princess was bored. She took to wandering through the countryside of the island of St Michael, enjoying the beautiful scenery and the warm sun.

One day, the princess looked up to find herself gazing into the face of a young man. He was a shepherd, but he was extremely handsome, with smokey green eyes. Perhaps it was not surprising that the princess found her steps took her to the young shepherd's hut more and more often. Here was someone who was not so wrapped up in his own world that he paid no attention to her. Before long, both the young people were deeply in love.

"What?" roared the king, when the princess asked his permission to marry a mere shepherd. "Not in a million years. You're going home on the next boat, my girl."

So, on her last day, the princess said goodbye to the shepherd. She returned to one side of the island and he to the other, but their thoughts were still together. They cried so bitterly that their tears formed two lagoons – one green from the eyes of the lovelorn shepherd, one blue from the eyes of the unfortunate princess. You can see them to this day.

THE PRINCESS
AND THE PEA

There was once a prince who wanted to get married, but he was determined to marry a real princess. As he went around the world in search of her, he found that there were very few real princesses to be found.

Back at their castle, his mother and father, the king and queen, tried to console him. But the prince was filled with gloom.

Outside, a storm was raging, so the family almost did not hear a banging at the great castle door. The king himself went to open it.

Outside, dripping wet, stood a very beautiful girl. "I am a princess," she said. "Could you possibly give me shelter tonight?"

Of course, the royal family invited her in, and as she warmed herself before the fire, it wasn't long before the prince began to feel more than a passing interest in the beautiful young visitor.

"But is she a *real* princess?" he whispered to his mother.

"We'll soon find out," replied the queen.

She ordered the servants to make up a bed for the princess, piled high with feather mattress after feather mattress. And under the bottom mattress, she placed a tiny dried pea.

The next morning, the lovely visitor joined the family for breakfast.

"Did you sleep well, my dear?" asked the queen with a shrewd look at the girl.

"I wish I could say that I did," replied the guest. "But I could feel something hard through the mattresses. I'm afraid I am black and blue this morning."

Then the queen knew that this was indeed a real princess, for only princesses have skin that is so delicate they can feel a pea through mountains of mattresses.

The princess and the prince were married and lived happily ever after. And the pea? Well, they say that if you visit the kingdom's poshest museum, you can see it for yourself!

THE TROLLS AND THE PUSSY CAT

In times gone by, trolls and humans got on pretty well together. Trolls would come and borrow things from the humans sometimes, but they always brought them back in good order.

However, there was one thing the trolls did that annoyed the villagers. On Christmas Eve, just as everyone was sitting down to a special family meal, the trolls would come in, drive out whichever unfortunate family they had chosen, and have their own Christmas meal at the table instead.

This went on year after year until, one snowy night just before Christmas, a man with a bear on a chain came knocking at the door of one house, asking if he could have a bed for the night.

The family agreed and even asked him to join their Christmas celebrations, but they warned him that there was a danger trolls would come in and they would all find themselves out in the snow.

"Oh, that doesn't worry me," said the man, and in he came.

After a splendid meal and singing and dancing (especially from the bear!) everyone went to bed. The bear and the man settled down in front of the fire.

Suddenly, in rushed the trolls. As they laid the table, one troll wandered over to the fire.

"Hello, pussy cat!" she cooed, and she bent down to stroke the furry animal.

"Grrrr!" Up leapt the bear, and he chased every single troll from the house.

Well, the next year, the trolls came around on Christmas Eve as usual. But before they came in, they shouted outside the door.

"Do you still have that large pussy cat?"

"Yes, and she now has seven kittens!" the head of the house called back.

"Then we'll leave you in peace this year," laughed the trolls. And they've been no trouble at all ever since!

THE BOY
AND THE MAGPIE

Once there was a poor boy called Olle. Although he had plenty to eat, warm clothes and a nice home, he was always moaning about other things he would like. "I wish I had a penknife," he said, "and a sledge, and a bike."

One day, Olle's grandfather got so fed up with hearing this that he told the boy, "Go into the forest and put salt on a magpie's tail. Then, if you wish quickly, you can have everything you want."

Olle went into the forest, not at all sure he would be able to get close to a magpie, but to his surprise, one of the birds spoke to him!

"I am really an enchanted prince," said the bird. "If you give me a fine penknife, I will be able to break the spell and give you everything your heart could desire."

So Olle went picking berries to sell in the town. When he had the money, he bought a penknife and hurried back to the forest.

"Hmm, I was thinking of something bigger," said the magpie. "Keep the knife.

What I want now is a really good sledge. Then you can have your wish."

Using his penknife, Olle began carving little toys and trinkets. With the money he got for these, he bought a sledge and set off back to the magpie.

"Hmm, I've changed my mind," said the bird. "Now I want a bicycle."

Off went Olle. With the sledge, he started making deliveries. He worked hard until he had enough money for a bicycle. Then he went back to find the magpie.

"Fair enough," said the cunning bird. "Sprinkle some salt on my tail and you can have your wish, but be quick!"

Olle did as he was told but … he couldn't think what to wish for! Everything he had dreamed of he already had through hard work and his own brains.

"Too late!" called the magpie, flying away, but Olle had learned a valuable lesson. He worked hard all his life and never wanted for anything.

HOW THE BEAR LOST ITS TAIL

Long ago, bears in the cold countries near the North Pole had long furry tails like foxes. They looked beautiful and all would have been well if bears had not also been both rather silly and very greedy. Well, a bear has a big tummy that needs to be filled!

One day, Bear was walking by a frozen lake when he came across Fox tucking into a large and delicious fish.

"Where did you get that?" asked Bear, licking his lips.

"In the lake, of course," said Fox, who had always enjoyed getting the better of his bigger friend. "You can catch one yourself. It's very easy. I'll show you how."

Fox led Bear out into the middle of the lake and showed him a little hole in the ice.

"Sit down and drop your tail through the ice," advised Fox. "Pretty soon a fish will come along and nibble your tail. As soon as you feel that, whip your tail out of the hole and you will have a fine fish."

Smiling to himself, Fox went on his way. Bear sat down and lowered his tail into the icy water. It was terribly cold, but, thought Bear, it was worth it for the pleasure of a big fish dinner.

Hour after hour, Bear sat and waited. Nothing nibbled at his tail at all. At last, as the moon rose in the sky, Bear decided he had had enough. It was time to go home.

But what was this? The hole had frozen over and Bear's tail was stuck fast. Bear grunted and groaned and pulled. At last, tumbling head over heels, he pulled himself free. Unfortunately, most of his tail was still in the lake.

So that is how great big bears came to have such short little tails. And foxes, who still have long, bushy tails, are smiling about that business to this very day.

FINLAND

ANDROCLES AND THE LION

Androcles was a slave with a very cruel master. Eventually, the boy could not stand his harsh treatment any longer. He ran away, even though he knew that he would be executed if was caught.

Hiding in a desert, where he hoped he would not be found, Androcles came to a large cave that might offer him shelter from the hot sun. He hurried inside.

But the cave was the den of a huge lion. It sprang from the shadows, roaring at the terrified boy. However, instead of attacking Androcles, the lion lay down and began to whimper, holding up its paw in a pitiful way.

Androcles could not bear to see another creature in pain. Bravely, he examined the lion's paw and found that there was a large thorn embedded in it. With great care, he removed the thorn and bound up the wound.

The slave and the lion lived together for a while, but eventually Androcles longed to see human beings again, so he headed to the nearest town. Unfortunately, almost as soon as he arrived, he was recognized and thrown into jail as a runaway. His fate was settled: the following day he would be thrown to the wild beasts in the local arena, while crowds of spectators watched and cheered.

The next day, Androcles walked into the arena with as much courage as he could manage. As a ferocious lion leapt towards him, he closed his eyes, ready for death.

But instead of sharp teeth and claws, he felt a rough tongue licking his face! It was his old friend, the lion from the cave, which had also been captured.

Seeing the man and the lion embracing each other with affection, the crowd called for them both to be saved. And the town's governor decreed that it should be so.

Androcles and the lion walked from the arena together, free at last.

THE BEGGARS AND THE GATE

 There was once a group of beggars who wandered about, living off the scraps that people threw away.

One day, the beggars happened to find a silver coin in the street.

"Now we can eat like everyone else," said one of them. "Let's order food for a feast and find a private place to enjoy it."

So the beggars ordered all kinds of good things to eat and even hired a porter to carry the feast out of the town.

Anxious not to be observed, in case envious people tried to steal their wonderful food, the beggars at last settled on a rather strange place for their picnic. It was a cemetery! Within the cemetery was a tomb that had a little garden all around it, with a wall all around that. The beggars peered in through the gate in the wall and decided that this was the perfect place.

Soon the food was all laid out on the ground and the porter was dismissed. The beggars settled down to enjoy their meal.

But after they had been eating for a few moments, one of the party noticed that the porter had left the gate open.

"Just get up and shut it, will you?" he asked one of his companions.

"No! You get up and shut it!" was the reply.

Finally, the beggars agreed that the next person to speak should shut the gate.

In silence they sat. Minute after minute passed. Suddenly, a pack of dogs rushed in. They seized the food and ate every crumb! Not one of the beggars said a word – in case he had to be the one to get up and shut the gate.

Then one dog, spotting some food lodged in a beggar's beard, hopped up and devoured it, nipping the beggar in the process.

"Ouch!" cried the beggar.

"Hah! Now you shut the gate!" laughed the others, but the bitten beggar sighed.

"Not much point," he said. "We no longer have anything that anyone would wish to steal!"

PEPELYOUGA AND THE GOLDEN SLIPPER

 Once there was a beautiful girl whose mother fell ill. "When I am dead, my daughter," said the woman, "I will still care for you. If ever you are in need, come to my grave and I will help you."

Before long, the woman died. All too soon, her husband married a widow, who also had a daughter. But the wife and her daughter were unkind. They made the lovely girl do all the work around the house and called her Pepelyouga, which means "cinders".

One day, as they got ready for church, the stepmother said, "Pepelyouga, you can't come. Pick up all this grain before we return or it will be the worse for you." So saying, she flung a basketful of grain all over the yard.

Pepelyouga was in despair, until she remembered her mother's words. She hurried to her grave and was astonished to see an open chest on it, containing three dresses.

On top were perched two doves. "Put on one of the dresses and go to church," chirped the doves. "We will pick up the grain for you."

So Pepelyouga put on a beautiful silk dress and set off. Everyone was amazed to see such a lovely young woman – especially a local nobleman who at once fell in love with her.

The stepmother and her daughter were furious. The next week they did the same thing, but Pepelyouga turned up in a gorgeous silver gown. When, the following week, she wore a wonderful gown of gold, the nobleman simply had to follow her. But the girl fled, leaving only a golden slipper behind.

The young man took the slipper and hunted everywhere for its owner. When he came to Pepelyouga's house, her stepmother hid her in a grain trough. "Do you have any more daughters?" asked the young man, when the stepdaughter had failed to fit the dainty shoe.

"No!" came the reply, but the rooster on the rooftop cried, "Cock-a-doodle-doo! What about the one in the grain trough?"

When he found Pepelyouga, the young nobleman was overjoyed. She became his wife and lived happily ever after.

THE GOLDEN STAG

Once there were two children who found themselves lost and alone in a great forest. Soon they were hungry and thirsty. Seeing some water pooled in the tracks of a fox, the boy knelt down to drink, but the little girl said, "No! Don't drink that! You might turn into a fox and run away. Who will look after me then?"

The two children walked further, until they saw some water pooled in the tracks of a bear. Once again, the little boy knelt down. But his sister cried, "No! What if you turn into a bear and attack me?"

On they went as before, until they came to the tracks of a massive stag. Once again, there was water shining in the prints. This time, nothing would stop the boy. He drank eagerly.

Before his sister's astonished eyes, the boy turned into a magnificent golden stag. From his shining antlers, jewels sparkled. Although he could no longer use a human voice, the stag told the girl she need not be afraid.

After that, the stag cared for his sister tenderly. He built her a nest high in a tree and brought her food each day. She grew into a very beautiful young woman, with long black hair and dark eyes.

One day, a prince came by and saw the girl. He knew at once that he must make her his wife. Back in his palace, he summoned a very wise old woman. The woman set out for the forest and pretended to be poor and in need of help. Feeling sorry for her, the girl climbed down from her tree and was captured.

When the golden stag returned and found her gone, he let out a great roar. He followed the footsteps of the old woman back to the royal palace.

Meanwhile, the girl had met the prince and decided that she would be quite happy married to him. When the magnificent stag was given a grand stable in the palace grounds, she was even happier.

THE CLEVER LITTLE KIDS

There was once a mother goat who had three kids. One day, she had to go out. Before she went, she said to her children, "Whatever you do, don't open the door to anyone but me. I'll bring you some milk when I come back."

The kids promised to do as she said.

The mother goat had not been gone very long when there came a knock at the door.

"Darlings, it's your mother with some lovely milk for you. Let me in!"

But the kids said, "You're not our mother. She has a nice, soft voice. Go away!"

A little while later, there came another knock on the door.

"Dear ones," called a nice, soft voice, "here I am, home again, bringing you some delicious milk. Open the door!"

"It sounds like our mother," said the kids, "but we must be sure."

"Stick your foot through the window," called the kids to the person outside.

In through the window came a foot. The kids looked at it suspiciously.

"Our mother doesn't have horrible black claws," they said. "Our mother has dainty, smooth hoofs. Go away, whoever you are!"

An hour or two passed and there was another knock at the door.

"Sweet ones, I'm home! Let me in!"

"It sounds like our mother," said one kid.

"It looks like our mother," said the second kid, peering out of the window.

"It is our mother!" chorused the three kids as they opened the door.

As they drank their delicious milk, the kids told their mother what had happened.

"Hmmm. That would be the big bad wolf," she said. "You did well, my children. How lucky I am to have such good and clever little kids!"

SMOK WAWELSKI AND THE SHOEMAKER

Long ago, the people of Krakow in Poland were troubled by a horrible dragon called Smok Wawelski. He ate anything he could lay his claws upon, including grain, cows, sheep … and even grannies! He really was a very unpleasant creature to have around.

At last, the King of Krakow could bear it no longer. "If anyone can find a way to rid us of this dragon," he said, "I will give him the hand of my daughter in marriage."

Well, various schemes were tried, but hideous Smok Wawelski put an end to them all, usually eating the experimenters in the process. The king was in despair.

Finally, a shoemaker's apprentice had an idea. He filled a huge sack with salt and left it outside the dragon's cave. Thinking it was a tasty snack, the dragon soon came out and gobbled it up. Luckily, the little shoemaker had the sense to keep out of the way.

Pretty soon, the dragon began to feel very, very thirsty. He waddled down to the Vistula River and began to drink. But he simply could not drink enough. Gulp after gulp of the fresh, cold water he took, and his huge tummy grew bigger and bigger and bigger, until suddenly … it burst!

So that was the end of Smok Wawelski. The king was true to his promise, and the young shoemaker married the princess. He couldn't believe his good luck, and she was very proud of her clever husband, so they lived happily together.

If you ever visit Krakow, find the dragon's cave at Wawel Castle and listen very carefully. In the whispers and echoes of the ancient walls you may hear the roars of the ghost of Smok Wawelski as he prowls around his cave.

THE CAT
AND THE ROOSTER

 Friendship can grow where you least expect it. Once upon a time, a cat and a rooster were great friends. They lived together in a little hut in the forest. The cat would play his fiddle, and the rooster would sing. They were pretty good!

Each day, the cat went out into the forest to find food. The rooster stayed at home.

"It's dangerous out there, my friend," the cat would say. "Promise me you will stay inside until I come back."

One morning, the rooster promised as usual, but when he opened the windows to breathe in the clean, spring air, he saw some delicious grain on the ground outside. He simply couldn't resist going out to taste it.

Well, the second the rooster stepped out of the door, a cunning old fox grabbed him and ran off into the forest.

"Help!" squawked the rooster, but there was no one to hear.

When the cat returned that evening, he noticed the grain lying on the ground and guessed what had happened.

Next morning, as soon as it was light, the cat set off for the fox's cottage.

"I hope I am not too late," gasped the cat, as he ran on silent paws through the trees.

The old fox was out hunting, but he had left his five children at home, warning them not to let anyone into the house. The rooster was trussed up in a corner, waiting for the fox to come home and start dinner.

The fox was cunning, but the cat was even cleverer.

"Dear children, your father warned you not to let anyone in, but he didn't say anything about you coming out!" he cried, and he played such a jolly tune on his fiddle that all the fox children came out to dance.

Then the cat caught them all in a sack and hurried inside to rescue the rooster. The two friends lived happily ever after.

Winterkölbl's Riddle

Once a poor woodcutter could no longer support his family, so he took his youngest daughter into the forest and left her there. The little girl was frightened and she tried to find her way home. Instead, she found, in a clearing, a strange little man who was boiling something in a large cauldron. As he danced around the bubbling pot, he sang:

Boil and bubble all the day
Who is this who comes my way?

The little girl forgot to be frightened and gratefully sat down for something to eat. She found that the little man lived within the trunk of a tree. He was kind to her, so she stayed and learned to cook and look after the funny little house. But the little man would never tell her his name.

One day, the little man took his adopted daughter to the royal palace.

"I have trained her well," he said. "She would make a fine servant for the queen."

The queen was delighted by the girl and treated her well. When the queen's son, the young king, came home, he was even more pleased. It was not long before he had fallen in love with the stranger and asked for her hand in marriage.

Rather to his surprise, the queen raised no objections. "We will," she said, "have to ask the girl's father, however."

The strange little man arrived at the palace with an odd little smile. "You have my blessing," he said, "if you can tell me my own name. Ha ha!"

Nobody could, but the clever queen followed the little man back to his home. Outside his house, as usual, was a huge cauldron. He sang as he danced around the steaming vessel:

Boil and bubble all the same,
No one will guess Winterkölbl is my name!

Of course, he was wrong. The young king and his new queen lived happily ever after.

THE HUNGRY, LAZY WOLF

 A ploughman was sitting on the headland one day, eating some bread for his lunch, when a hungry wolf came along. Being a kindly man (and a wise one, too), the ploughman shared his snack with the wolf.

"Well, that was really delicious," said the wolf, licking his lips. "What would I have to do to make bread like that?"

"It's pretty easy," said the ploughman. "First you plough the land, as I have been doing. Then you plant some grain. Then you wait until it comes up, being careful to scare off the crows and pull out any weeds. When it is tall and golden, you have to cut it down and thresh it. After that, you need to grind the corn. Finally, you mix it with yeast and wait while it rises. Then you put it in the oven to bake. When that is done, you simply wait until the bread is cool … and eat it!"

The wolf looked at the ploughman in disgust. "There has to be an easier way of getting something to eat than that!" he said.

So the wolf set off to find some easy food, and at last he came across a horse in a field. By now, he was hungry enough to eat a horse!

"I'm going to eat you!" snarled the wolf, looking as menacing as he knew how.

"One moment," said the horse, "let me take my iron shoes off first. They would give you terrible indigestion."

So the horse took off her shoes, and as she did so, she kicked the wolf hard in the head, until he didn't feel like eating a horse after all.

Next day, the wolf found a ram in a meadow. "I'm going to eat you all up!" he said.

"Really?" said the ram. "I'm pretty old and tough, but if you're sure. I tell you what, I'll jump right into your mouth myself to make it easier for you."

The ram leapt … and he knocked the wolf out cold. It was three days before he came round. After that, the wolf knew that there was no such thing as an easy lunch!

THE FOOL AND THE EMPTY BARN

Once there was a farmer who had three sons. The two eldest were clever lads who did what their father told them, but the youngest went his own way and never showed what he could do. His father told him that he was a fool.

The farmer decided that it was time to reward his hardworking sons, so he asked them to help him build a huge barn. When it was finished, he said, "Whoever can fill this barn in a day will become its owner."

The first son thought hard. He thought about the largest thing on the farm. Then off he went to fetch the carthorse, which was a huge and powerful animal. But when, with much coaxing and many apples, the horse was persuaded into the barn, it was obvious that it only took up one small corner. It didn't begin to fill the building.

The second son also thought about what would take up a lot of space. He went out to the haystack and carted all the hay into the barn. He piled it up so that it reached the roof – almost. There was still quite a lot of space in the barn.

"Well, are you going to try, Fool?" the farmer asked his youngest son.

"In an hour or two," replied the boy.

An hour or so later, when the barn was empty once more of horses and hay, the farmer and his first two sons waited by the doorway for the youngest son to have a go. The boy wandered into the barn as if he didn't have a care in the world. Then, from his pocket, he took out a small stub of candle and a flint. He struck a spark from the flint and lit the candle. Then he placed it in the middle of the floor and went back to the doorway. At once, from one small flame, the barn was filled with light – and the so-called fool won the contest.

LATVIA

49

ASIA

THE OLD MAN AND THE BEAR

 Once an old man went to sow some turnip seeds. He worked hard all day but just as he was about to cast his seeds on to the tilled ground, a huge bear rushed out of the forest, growling furiously.

"Don't hurt me! Don't hurt me!" cried the old man.

"Give me one good reason why not," grunted the bear.

"If you help me to sow these seeds," said the old man quickly, "we will have a wonderful harvest. Then, you shall have all the green tops and I will only take the roots."

The bear, knowing no better, agreed. When the time came to harvest the turnips, the old man filled his cart with the roots and, true to his word, gave the tops to the bear.

The bear ate the tops, but just as the old man was ready to set out for the city to sell his turnips, the bear began to wonder.

"Let me just taste one of those old roots," he said.

Well, the moment the bear tasted the turnips, he roared with anger.

"You tricked me!" he cried. "These roots are the best part of the plant."

The following year, the old man thought it would be better not to risk a turnip crop, so he planted rye instead. A fine field of the grain grew in the summer sun. Then, just as the old man prepared to cut the rye, the bear once more came rushing out of the trees.

"Old man!" he yelled. "This time I will not be fooled. Share your crop with me!"

"It will be a great pleasure," said the old man. "And this time, good bear, I will take the tops and you can have the roots."

Well, the bear took the roots and carried them back into the forest, but when he tried to chew them, he threw them down in disgust. This was no kind of food.

When the bear realized he had been tricked, he snarled and rolled his eyes. From that day to this, bears and men have never been friends.

THE RAVEN AND THE WATER OF LIFE

 When the Earth was young, Erleg Khaan brought death and disease into the world. From that day, every living thing, from the tallest tree to the smallest insect, must one day sicken and die. And that was true of humans, too.

Flying high over creation, the Raven saw all this and felt sorrow for the suffering people below. He decided to try to help.

Now, there was a mighty mountain named Humber Ula. It was the highest thing on Earth. And at the very top of Humber Ula was something higher still – an aspen tree with golden leaves. At the foot of the shining tree was a sparkling spring, and its water was the water of life. If any creature drank from the sacred spring, it would live for ever.

The Raven flew up, up, up to the top of Humber Ula. He fluttered down to the place where the precious crystal drops of water welled from the Earth. Then he took just one tiny beakful of the water of life. He knew that even this minute amount would be enough to give human beings immortality.

Holding the water carefully in his beak, the Raven flew back to the world of men. As he approached the place where the early humans had their camp, he felt his heart lift at the thought of the great gift he was bringing.

Suddenly, just as the dark shadow of the Raven fell upon the settlement below, an owl called out from a grove of pine trees nearby. Startled, the Raven opened his beak – and out fell the precious diamond drops, right onto the pine trees beneath.

And that is why to this day humans, like oak and ash trees, grow old and wither and one day die, but pine trees stay green even in the deepest winter, touched by the magic of the water of life.

AMIN AND THE UNPAID BILL

There was once a very poor man called Amin. He struggled to make a living on his tiny plot of land. One year, there was a dreadful drought. This was the end for Amin. He realized that there was no way he could survive the winter.

Amin went to the man next door, a merchant, and persuaded him to let him have a dozen eggs, for which he would, he said, pay later. Then, with the eggs to keep him going on his journey, Amin set off to seek his fortune.

Nothing was heard of Amin for seven years. Then, one fine morning, the excited villagers heard the news that Amin had returned. He was now a wealthy man, with horses, jewels, money and fine clothes.

It occurred to the merchant who had given Amin the eggs that he never had been paid for them. It also occurred to him that this might be a chance to make some money. He sent a bill to the rich man.

Well, Amin had been expecting the bill, but he hadn't been expecting the amount. The merchant wanted five hundred silver pieces! Naturally, Amin thought that was a bit pricey for a dozen eggs. He refused to pay.

The merchant brought the matter before the judge. "Those twelve eggs might have hatched into hens and cockerels," he said. "They, in turn, might have produced more. By now, Amin could have become a wealthy poultry owner. Indeed, for all I know, that's exactly what happened!"

"That sounds reasonable," said the judge. "Do you have anything to say, Amin?"

"Sorry, Judge," said Amin. "I'm a little out of breath. I rushed here after planting a plate of boiled beans in my garden. I hope for a bumper crop next year."

"Don't be ridiculous!" said the judge. "Boiled beans won't grow. Are you mad?"

"As mad as a man who thinks I could make a fortune from poultry hatched from twelve *hardboiled* eggs," said Amin mildly.

The case was dismissed.

THE SULTAN
AND THE BEGGARS

There was once a sultan who liked to make a show of charitable deeds. He wasn't really interested in doing good, but he liked to be thought a generous and virtuous man.

Each day, two beggars were brought before the sultan, who magnanimously handed each of them a small loaf of bread.

"Thanks be to the great and good sultan!" cried one beggar.

"Thanks be to God!" cried the other.

After a while, this began to get on the sultan's nerves.

"I give you the bread, not God," he said peevishly to the devout beggar. "Why don't you thank *me*?"

"Without God's goodness, you wouldn't have the wealth to do so," replied the beggar.

The sultan couldn't think of a reply to this, so he decided to make his point in another way. He told his baker to put some jewels in one loaf of bread and leave the other plain. The next morning, he was careful to hand the loaf with the jewels hidden inside to the beggar who always thanked him for his generosity.

But when he was handed his loaf, the first beggar thought it looked a bit lumpy. He pretended to stumble, so that he knocked into the other beggar and they both dropped their loaves. Then he was careful to pick up the loaf that looked less lumpy.

"Thanks be to the great and good sultan!" cried the foolish beggar.

"Thanks be to God!" cried the other, breaking open the loaf and seeing the gems sparkling inside.

The sultan was not a stupid man. "All right, you win!" he muttered under his breath to someone that nobody present could see. And to the assembled court he cried, "Thanks be to God!" And he meant it.

55

KHALID AND THE STRANGE BERRIES

Well over a thousand years ago, a young boy was herding goats in the dry lands of what is now Saudi Arabia. His name was Khalid. As the day wore on, he grew tired and sat down. The goats, too, became sleepy. While the sun was high in the sky, the boy slept, confident that his goats would also be snoozing the afternoon away.

As the evening began to cool, the boy awoke. There were his goats, looking fresh and lively – just as they would after a good sleep.

Day after day, the same thing happened. Then, one morning, the boy stumbled over a stone and hurt his knee. It wasn't a bad graze, but it felt a little uncomfortable – too sore for the young shepherd to fall asleep as usual.

So, feeling a little sorry for himself, Khalid watched his goats, and to his surprise, they did not go to sleep at all. In fact, they spent the whole afternoon jumping and running like kids. How could they be so lively? Khalid could think of no explanation as he pulled his lunch of bread and dates from his bag.

After some food, Khalid felt much better. He wondered if perhaps it was something the goats were eating that was making them so frisky. But what could it be?

Khalid began to watch the goats carefully. He noticed that they often nibbled at the berries of an evergreen bush that grew in that area. The boy had no idea what the bush was, but he was intrigued and began to experiment with the berries himself.

No one knows what gave him the idea of roasting the seeds inside the berries, grinding them up, and steeping them in hot water, but when he tasted the brew he had made, Khalid found that, like the goats, he felt full of energy. Today people everywhere feel the same, but young Khalid had no idea that he was the very first person to taste … coffee.

MUSHKIL GUSHA'S MAGIC

There was once an old woodcutter who went every day to the desert to collect thornbushes to sell in the market. One day, his daughter said to him, "Father, could you buy us something special today? Some date cakes would be good."

Wishing to please his daughter, the man worked even harder that day to gather more thornbushes to make more money at the market. He did as he had planned, but it was so late when he got home that the girl had already bolted the door, and the woodcutter had to sleep on the doorstep.

The next morning, the woodcutter woke with the dawn. It would be silly to wait here until my daughter wakes, he thought. I'll go straight off to work and see her tonight.

Once again, the woodcutter worked very hard. So hard, in fact, that once again the door was bolted when he got home. For another long night, he slept on the doorstep.

The next morning, the woodcutter once again awoke very early and set off to work. Unfortunately, he made the same mistake for the third time. As he sat on the ground, feeling sorry for himself, a dervish in a long, green robe suddenly appeared before him. The woodcutter was so tired and fed up that he poured out the whole story to the stranger.

"Do you know what day it is today?" the dervish asked the woodcutter.

"Why, yes, it is Friday," said the man.

"Indeed," said the dervish, sharing some food with the woodcutter. "It is the eve of our holy day. This is the time of Mushkil Gusha, the Remover of Difficulties. If you think a moment, you will realize that you are a fortunate man. If you wish to continue in your good luck, all you have to do is to find someone to share your excellent fortune with every Friday evening, and tell them about Mushkil Gusha."

At that moment, the door opened, and the man's daughter exclaimed with joy at the sight of her father. But the dervish was nowhere to be seen.

THE MAN WHO COUNTED HIS CHICKENS

After many long years of hoping, a woman was finally able to tell her husband that she was expecting a baby. He was delighted. "It will be a boy," he said confidently, "and he will be handsome, brave and clever."

The woman frowned. "There was once a dervish," she said, "who saved up the honey that his employer gave him in a great jar, which he carried around on his head. One day, realizing that the jar was almost full, he decided to sell it at the market. The honey would bring a good price. 'With the money I get,' said the dervish to himself, 'I will buy a few sheep. They will be sure to do well and produce fine lambs. Within, say, four years, I shall have over a hundred sheep. Then I'll be

able to buy some cattle, too, and become a respected farmer. The cattle will flourish. I'll buy a big house and find a lovely bride. She will give me many fine sons, who will keep me in my old age. I will sit in my garden and be happy all day long.' In his excitement, the dervish waved his stick enthusistically in the air … and broke the honey jar."

The father-to-be frowned. "What has that to do with anything?" he asked impatiently.

"Having children is a difficult business," said his wife. "You don't know if our child will be born safely. You don't know if it will be a boy. You don't know if he (if it is a he) will be brave or clever or handsome. You have no idea

whether he will bring great riches to our family. Don't tempt fate with talk like that, husband. Remember what King Solomon said: 'Don't boast, for you never know what the next day will bring.'"

THE SINGER OF LOVE SONGS

There was once a rich merchant who employed many people. One of them was a young man called Zarief, who was as handsome as he was clever. In every way, he was a fine young man.

One day, the merchant sent his daughter to deliver a message to the place where Zarief worked. The young man fell deeply in love with the girl at first glance, but they had little chance to talk.

Shortly afterwards, Zarief had to make a delivery to his master's home. He met the lovely girl again and discovered that her name was Ataba.

It was not the custom for young men and women to be able to spend time alone together, so Zarief thought long and hard and finally decided that he would have to ask his master for his daughter's hand in marriage.

Well, the merchant laughed. "What do you have to offer her?" he cried. "I'm looking for a much better match for my precious girl.

But, if you want to show me you have a bit of initiative, go and bring me the finest grapes in the whole country."

Zarief did just that. It was a hard journey, especially for a penniless young man, but he was true to his word and brought back the very best grapes for his master. It was not, however, enough. After that, the merchant found test after test for the young man. He had to bring back the best oranges, dates, and many other kinds of goods from far and wide.

Wherever he went, Zarief dreamed of Ataba, and he found himself singing songs about her, telling of the troubles he had endured and the way in which love made it all worthwhile. Soon, hundreds of people had heard of the story of Zarief and Ataba.

At last, a friend that Zarief had made in Egypt went to the merchant and vouched for the young man. "Well, I must say I'm impressed by him," said the merchant. "The marriage can go ahead." And so it did. That was long ago, but to this day, Zarief's songs are sung at weddings in many countries.

THE MONKEYS
AND THE MOON

There was once a family of monkeys who lived near a ruined temple. They liked to think that they were wise, but the case was sadly otherwise.

One night, the leader of the monkeys happened to look into an old, abandoned well. Far, far below, in the still water, something white was shining.

"Look! Look!" cried the monkey. "The moon has fallen into the well! We must fish it out or we will never see moonlight again!"

It didn't occur to a single one of the silly monkeys to look up into the sky to see if the moon really had disappeared.

The monkeys gathered to discuss how they could rescue the moon. One of them suggested getting a long, long stick to fish it out. This seemed a very good idea. But although the monkeys found the longest branches they could in the forest, they were not long enough to reach the water at the bottom of the well.

"One of us will have to climb down and get it," said a young monkey. "But I'm not big and strong enough." Looking at the smooth sides of the well and seeing how very, very far

down the water was, the leader of the monkeys wisely (for once) decided that no single monkey was strong enough.

"We need to work together," he said.

So one monkey grabbed hold of a stout branch above the well, and one by one the monkeys made a living chain that reached down into the well.

"Almost there!" called the leader of the monkeys, who was at the very end of the chain. "Stretch!"

At that moment, the branch high above broke with the weight of all the monkeys. With a splash, they tumbled one after the other into the water and were never seen again.

But, as the dark water became still once more, the moon again shone in its depths – and high above in the night sky, too.

THE BRIGHT BLUE JACKAL

Jackals, as you may know, are always poking their noses in where they don't belong. They're hoping to find food without having to work for it.

One day, a particularly lazy jackal was wandering along when he saw a huge pot sitting in a yard. Inside was something that the jackal hoped was soup. He couldn't reach it from the ground, so he climbed up onto the edge of the pot.

Now jackals are fairly nimble, but they are not built for climbing. With a wail, the jackal overbalanced and fell right into the pot. As he clambered out, dripping, it soon became clear that the pot had not been full of soup at all. It was a huge batch of indigo dye. The jackal was bright blue all over.

The jackal lay down in the sun until he was dry. He was not at all sure what to do. Just then he saw a peacock, which was also bright blue, wandering past. He remembered that peacocks are sometimes kept in grand gardens because they are so beautiful. He was pretty sure that meant they got fed by the owners of the gardens. This seemed like a good idea for a hungry jackal.

So the blue jackal wandered off with his head in the air and soon ran into some old friends – who laughed.

"I've never seen a blue jackal!" scoffed one.

"You still haven't," said the jackal. "I'm not a jackal. I'm a peacock."

"Really?" said one friend. "I thought peacocks had gorgeous tails. Do you?"

"Er … no," said the jackal.

"And they have a mournful but tuneful cry," said another friend. "Do you?"

The jackal tried. His cry was neither tuneful nor mournful, although it did, in one sense, make you want to cry.

"Well, you say you are not a jackal," said another animal. "And you are certainly not a peacock. You are no-one at all. And we can't talk to no-one. Goodbye!"

THE FOOLISH SON

There was once a couple who had one son. He was not very clever, or very funny, or very athletic, or even very kind. In fact, his father despaired of him.

"You're wrong," said the boy's mother. "He will surprise you yet. I know our boy has it in him to do something really brilliant."

"Frankly, I doubt it," replied the father, "and I may as well tell you that I have no intention of finding a wife for such a useless son. But, if you insist, I'll give him one last chance. I've thought of a test."

Then the father gave his son a very small coin. "Take this to market," he said, "and use it to buy something to eat, something to drink, something to plant and something for the cow. You'll only be able to afford one thing, mind."

The boy set off, but when he came to the river, he sat down in despair. How on earth could he buy all that stuff with one tiny coin? Just then, the blacksmith's daughter came by. When she heard of the boy's trouble, she laughed. "Buy a watermelon," she said. "It will give you flesh to eat, juice to drink, seeds to plant and the rind to feed to the cow."

The boy was delighted. He ran to the market, bought a watermelon, and hurried home. His parents were delighted, too, and when they heard what had happened, they invited the blacksmith and his family to dinner. It was soon pretty clear that the boy and the clever girl had fallen in love, and a match was made.

"However," said the father that night to his wife, as they prepared for bed, "that boy still hasn't done anything brilliant, you know. It was the girl's idea."

"Oh yes, he has!" laughed the mother. "He has done something very brilliant indeed. He has found himself an excellent wife – as you did, dear husband!"

UNITY IS STRENGTH

The doves of the air loved to flock together like one big family. And when it came to looking for food, sometimes the more birds there were to search, the better it was.

One day, the doves found it hard to find food. They flew for miles over fields and gardens but could see nothing on the parched earth. At last, the youngest dove's sharp little eyes spotted some rice lying on the ground. The whole flock swooped down to enjoy it.

But no sooner had the birds landed than a net fell over them. It had been a trap! In vain, the birds struggled. The mesh of the net was too small to let even the youngest dove through.

Then the king of the doves spoke up. "Stop struggling!" he cried. "If we all take hold of the net in our beaks and fly up together, we shall surely be strong enough to rise into the air and escape.

At a signal from the king, each dove took hold of the net and flapped its wings. The hunters approaching from below were amazed to see the doves flying away, holding the net that still surrounded them.

The king directed the doves to fly to a nearby hillside where a friend of his lived. It was a little mouse, who was only too happy to nibble through the net and set the beautiful birds free.

You will still see doves flocking together to this day, for they have learned the lesson that their wise king taught them – that unity is strength.

63

Why the Gibbon Calls

There was once a prince called Chantakorop who, as was the custom, was sent to a hermit in the rainforest to learn wisdom. Chantakorop was not much of a scholar, but life was made bearable by the presence of the hermit's daughter, the beautiful Mora.

When it was time for the prince to return to his kingdom, the hermit presented him with a large clay pot. "This is my parting gift to you," said the hermit, "but whatever you do, don't open it until you reach your home. If you open it sooner, bad luck will befall you."

The prince thanked the hermit and set off for home, but each day, the pot seemed to get heavier and heavier, and the prince became more and more curious. At last, he could bear it no longer. He broke open the pot.

You can imagine his delight when the lovely Mora stepped from the pot, as if by magic. The prince was delighted to see her and lost no time in marrying her in the very next village he came to. The rest of the journey was very pleasant for both of them.

But as the prince neared the border of his own country, a bandit leapt out of the trees and challenged the prince to fight for the girl by his side.

Perhaps Chantakorop feared that this was the ill luck the hermit had mentioned. In any case, he was no match for the bandit, who struck the prince's sword from his hand.

"If you love me, throw me my sword," the prince called to his wife. But Mora, full of fear, hesitated just too long. With a cry, the bandit thrust his own sword into the unarmed man, who was instantly killed.

It is said that the hermit, using his ancient magic, turned Mora into a gibbon to save her from the bandit, and that ever since her mournful cries for her husband are heard through the forest.

THE GOD
WHO GREW

One day, an unmarried woman found a giant footprint in her garden. Curious, she placed her own foot in the giant print. In that moment, something very strange happened to her, and a few months later, she gave birth to a baby, whom she called Gióng.

But the baby boy was not like others. As he grew older, he neither walked nor spoke.

Then, one day, a messenger arrived to bring news that the land was in great trouble from an attacking army.

"Bring the messenger to me," said the baby. It was the first time he had spoken.

When the messenger arrived, Gióng said more. He demanded a huge suit of armour, an enormous sword, and a great horse made of iron. So powerful were his words that the messenger was in no doubt that this was a god in human form. He hurried off to do as he had been told.

"But my son," said his mother, "you are so small. How will you ever wear such huge and heavy armour?"

"Bring me food," said the baby.

After that, Gióng ate and ate and ate. He was soon the size of a grown man, but he didn't stop. By the time the armour arrived, he had reached a giant size, and it fit him perfectly. The sword, which twelve ordinary men could barely lift, was just right for him.

Then Gióng set about his country's enemies and triumphantly overthrew them. His iron horse came alive and trampled the enemies underfoot. Gióng fought so hard that even his mighty sword broke in two and he had to pull up a massive bamboo and swipe at all before him with that.

When he had finished, Gióng spurred on his iron steed and threw off his armour and helmet. The horse rose into the sky, taking the god back to the heavens from which he came. But they say that the hoofprints of the mighty horse can still be seen in Thailand.

JOJI AND THE TEMPLE CAT

Joji loved only one thing – drawing. And what is more, he only ever drew one thing – cats. As a baby, Joji drew cats in the earth with his chubby finger. As a young boy, he scribbled them on the walls with a stick of charcoal. His father, who was a farmer, shook his head. "That boy will never be interested in working on the land," he said. "Maybe he could be a priest."

Joji was sent to the temple to learn to be a priest. All the other boys listened carefully to their lessons. When the time came for them to learn to write, they made careful brushstrokes on their paper. But Joji wasn't interested in writing. As soon as he had a brushful of ink in his hand, he began to draw the slinky, silky curves of a cat. He had never been happier.

Day after day, Joji drew cats. He drew crouching cats, creeping cats, pouncing cats and sleeping cats. He drew them everywhere.

Of course, it wasn't long before the priests told Joji he would have to leave. But the boy did not dare to go home. Instead, he went to another temple nearby for shelter. There was no one about – just a huge room surrounded by white paper screens. Before he slept, Joji had covered every one of those screens with an enormous picture of a cat.

That night, Joji was awakened by an awful noise. Something was scratching and snuffling towards him. Suddenly, in the darkness, there was a thud and a cry. Then all was silence.

In the morning, Joji found a huge rat – as big as a cow – dead on the floor. What had killed it? Suddenly, Joji noticed that his cat on the paper screens was facing the other way, as if it had jumped down from the wall and jumped back up again.

"My cat saved my life," said Joji. "I will never stop drawing." And it is just as well that he didn't, for he became a famous artist, whose pictures are admired all over the world. They are, of course, of … cats.

THE YOUNGEST, WISEST WIFE

 Once there was a man whose wife had died. His household consisted of his four sons and the wives of the three eldest boys. These girls were constantly pestering the old man for permission to visit their home village.

"All right," said the old man at last. "You can go if you bring me back three presents: a flame wrapped in paper, a wind wrapped in paper, and music coming from the wind. If you can't do this, don't come back."

The girls were so excited to be going that they set off without thinking. When the impossibility of their task finally struck them, they sat down and began to cry.

"Can I help at all?" asked a young girl, passing on a water buffalo. She looked so kind and sympathetic that the wives soon found themselves telling her everything.

"I think I can help you," said the girl.

When the young wives returned home a few days later, the old man was ready to send them away. "Where are my presents?" he roared.

The first wife knelt before him. "Here is a paper lantern, great father," she said, "with a flame inside."

Next it was the second wife's turn. "Here is a paper fan, great father," she said. She flapped the fan, and the wind blew on the old man's face.

Finally, the third wife knelt down. She didn't say a word, but held up some little brass chimes. In the wind from the fan, they tinkled and made sweet music.

The old man knew when he was beaten. "Who told you how to do this?" he asked. When he heard about the young girl on the buffalo, he made up his mind at once that she would be a perfect wife for his youngest son. And what is more, with such a wise head on young shoulders, and in the absence of an older woman, she should be the head of the household. Which just shows that he was pretty wise as well.

CHINA

67

THE STRONGEST MAN IN THE WORLD

Badang was a poor man. In fact, he was a slave, having to do his master's bidding day and night. He was powerless, unable to escape or better his lot.

Even when Badang tried to do something for himself, he was unlucky. In his tiny amount of free time, he liked to set fish-traps on the seabed. But time after time, when the slave opened his traps, he found that inside there were only bones and half-eaten fish.

Badang was not a man to give up easily. He decided to lie in wait and see what was eating his catch. He hid among some trees by the shore and waited patiently.

The fish-thief, when he came, was like nothing and no one that Badang had ever seen before. He was a huge, ugly monster, larger than any man. He had glaring red eyes, rough hair and beard, horns on his head and tusks protruding from his jaw.

As Badang watched, the monster raided his fish-traps, wolfing down all his catch.

At that moment, Badang could bear it no longer. Leaping from the trees, he grabbed the creature and held his machete to its throat.

"Only let me go," gasped the monster, "and I will grant you any wish in the world."

Badang thought of everything he had to endure in his miserable life.

"Only make me strong," he said, "stronger than any man alive, and I will be happy."

Sure enough, when Badang went to push the monster from him, he found that he had acquired the strength of twenty men. It was not long before his fame spread far and wide. Soon, rich and powerful people were queuing up to see his powers. A nearby king asked him to push a huge wooden boat down to the sea. Even a thousand men together could not shift it. Badang did it with ease.

The king was so impressed that he made Badang commander of his army. And the once-powerless slave became the second most powerful man in the land.

THE FOUNDING OF THE LION CITY

Hundreds of years ago, Prince Sang Nila Utama lived a charmed life. What we now call Indonesia was at peace, and the prince spent his days with his friends, hunting, feasting and singing.

But there came a time when the prince tired of his usual activities. He decided to set off in search of adventure. Sailing from island to island, he went where the wind took him and saw many new and strange things.

One day, the prince looked out across the sea and saw a new island. He was told that it was called Temasek.

"I must go there!" he declared. "I cannot rest until I set foot on that island."

The captain protested, for he could see that a storm was brewing, but the young man insisted. Sure enough, when they were halfway to the island, the winds blew, and mighty waves crashed over the boat.

In desperation, the captain ordered his men to throw all the cargo overboard, so that the boat would not sink. It was no good.

Finally, the captain turned to his noble passenger. "My Lord, throw your crown overboard," he begged, "or we shall all perish."

Sang Nila Utama's crown was made of gold and jewels. Reluctantly, he threw it into the boiling sea. Amazingly, the boat began to ride the waves, and eventually, the storm abated and the passengers reached their island.

It was beautiful, bright with flowers and birds. Suddenly, as he walked along the silvery sands, the prince saw an animal he had never met before. It was large, fierce and magnificent. The prince's companions told him it was a lion.

"Then I will call this place *Singa Pura*, the Lion City," said Sang Nila Utama, "and I will rule it myself."

He did, and the city of Singapore flourishes to this day.

THE FROG IN THE WELL

Once there was a little frog who lived at the bottom of a deep, deep well. He had cool water to drink. He had insects to eat. By day, he could see the blue sky above. By night, he could see the stars and the silvery moon. He was very happy with his life.

But sometimes, birds flying overhead would call down to the frog. "Won't you come up here and see what the wide world is like? It is bigger and more beautiful than you can imagine."

"No, thank you," the frog would reply. "I am quite happy down here. Why don't you come down and see how nice it is?"

But no one ever wanted to visit the little frog's dark home, and they soon got fed up of his refusal to explore the world.

One day, a little yellow bird decided she must take the frog under her wing. She flew down into the well, scooped up the surprised amphibian, and carried him off on her back.

"Ow!" cried the little frog. "It is so bright out here, I can't see! Oh, but wait a minute, what's that big blue thing? What's that tall white thing? What are all these shimmering shapes of green?"

"Those are leaves!" laughed the bird. "And that is the sea and that is a mountain. Aren't they big? Aren't they beautiful?"

"Let me down!" cried the little frog, and he hopped off to see the world for himself. Of course, it was bigger and more beautiful than he could ever have guessed. He found a deep blue pool with lilies on it and lived there very happily ever after. And, although he had once believed himself happy in his old, dark well, he never went back to it again.

THE TIGER AND THE TOAD

One day a tiger fell into a pit and found he was trapped. He roared and raved but he could not get out.

Just then, a man passed by. He felt sorry for the tiger, but he was a little wary of helping so ferocious an animal.

"Just put a branch down into the pit and I will be able to jump out," said the tiger. "I promise I won't harm you."

So the man did as the tiger asked. Out leaped the tiger, showing his sharp teeth.

"Silly man! I'm hungry now and my dinner will be … YOU!" growled the tiger.

"That's not fair!" the man protested.

At that moment, a croaky voice was heard from a nearby stone. It was a toad.

"What a noise!" he said. "Show me what exactly happened. I don't understand."

"Well," grunted the tiger, "I was in the pit … like this." He jumped back in.

"Only," said the man thoughtfully, "this wasn't here then." And he took out the big branch he had placed in the pit.

"I see," said the toad. "Well, I suggest that we leave matters exactly as they are now. Go on your way, my man, and try to think before you act in the future."

The man gratefully hurried off, while the tiger growled and spat in the pit.

The toad peered over the edge. "That's quite enough from you, ungrateful creature," he said. "A promise is a promise, and you must learn to keep yours!"

THE TEMPLE ON THE HILL

Long ago, the capital of the Khmer empire of Cambodia was at Angkor, and the present capital, Phnom Penh, was just a tiny village. Some say the change came because of the story you are about to read.

In the tiny village I mentioned lived a lady called Penh. Although her house was on top of a hill, when the Mekong River overflowed its banks, the floodwaters rushed right past her doors. One day, she was startled to find that a huge tree trunk had been swept by the water right into her house.

There were more surprises in store. When Lady Penh looked more carefully at the trunk, she found it was hollow. Inside were four bronze statues of the Buddha.

Lady Penh gazed at the statues, and a feeling of peace came over her. She decided that the statues deserved a new home and paid for a temple, called a *wat*, to be built next to her house. It wasn't long before people began to visit the temple in their thousands. Everyone seemed to feel that the statues and their temple were somehow special. Soon, the temple became a place of pilgrimage.

The popularity of the temple and the mysterious appearance of the statues made some people feel that the gods were calling for a new home in Cambodia. When an army from Thailand invaded the country and attacked Angkor, it was decided to move the capital to a new place. A site was chosen near the temple with the four statues.

And that is how the capital got its name, for *phnom* means "hill" in the Khmer language, and *Phnom Penh* means "Lady Penh's Hill". The temple that sits at its heart is called the *Wat Phnom*, or "hill temple". Some people believe it is the very same temple that Lady Penh built all those years ago, after the river's gift came to her door.

THE COCONUT
COLLECTOR

One day, a man set out with his horse to collect coconuts. He worked hard all day, until his horse was so loaded that not a single extra coconut could be added.

The man decided to take a different route home, which he thought might be easier for the horse with the heavy load, but he was less familiar with it than his usual way. As he set out, he saw a boy by the side of the road.

"Hey, boy!" he called, "I live over that way. How long will it take me to get home?"

The boy thought for a while and looked with interest at the heavily laden horse before he replied. Then he said, "Well, it depends if you hurry or if you go slowly. If you hurry, it will take you a long time. If you go slowly, you'll soon be home."

The man shook his head impatiently. "You're talking nonsense, boy," he said. And he went on his way. It seemed obvious to him that if he hurried, he would get home more quickly, so he urged on his horse.

The poor old horse did its best. It broke into a ragged trot – and coconuts began to break free from their bags and nets and go bouncing all over the pathway. Over and over again, the man had to stop and pick them up. Then, conscious that he had lost time, he would push his horse on again – and the same thing would happen. The man must have stopped to pick up coconuts hundreds of times.

At last, frustrated beyond belief, the man stood by the side of the road and scratched his head. He remembered what the boy had said. Certainly, going quickly was taking a very long time indeed.

"All right, old friend," the man told his horse, "take it at your own pace."

Slowly, the horse plodded on, being careful not to drop a single coconut. It was not very long at all before the man and his horse and his coconuts arrived safely home.

AFRICA

AN EARTHLY PARADISE

Once there was a king who had everything this world can offer. He was rich in jewels, palaces and lands, but he also had a wife who loved him and children of whom any man could be proud. But it was not enough for him. He felt that there was something missing.

One day, the king found an ancient book. It described a wonderful place called Paradise, where good people lived after they died. The king longed to find himself in such a place, where flowers bloomed, and birds sang, and all was happiness and love.

"With all my wealth and power," he said, "I can surely build my own Paradise."

The king summoned his advisers and set to work. He ordered palaces to be built, with walls of jewels and perfumed halls. The palaces were surrounded by gardens, where the most beautiful flowers bloomed, crystal drops of water danced in the air above marble fountains, and brightly feathered birds sang sweetly among the shady trees.

For years, the king worked on his great project – and all his subjects worked too. The scheme was so absorbing that the king didn't even notice when his loving wife died and his children left to follow their own dreams.

At last the king felt that his Paradise on earth was finished. Dressed in the finest silken robes, with jewels on his fingers and rose petals beneath his feet, the king walked for the first time in his finished Paradise.

Suddenly, the sound of birdsong died away. The ground began to shake. The king watched in horror as his earthly Paradise tumbled into a great chasm in the ground. Before his eyes, the king's great dream fell in ruins. Finally, the king himself was swallowed up. Of his great enterprise, all that was left was the shifting sand, ceaselessly sighing in the desert wind.

THE RETURN OF THE WATERS OF LIFE

Without water, there can be no life. In Egypt, it is the River Nile that, every year, floods the land with precious water and makes it fertile.

But once, long ago, there was a time when, for seven years, the Nile did not flood. Crops died. Animals died. People died. The ruler of the land was desperate. He turned to his priests and begged them to make offerings to Hapi, the god of the river, before the whole land returned to desert.

The chief priest set off for the island of Elephantine, where the monkey-headed god Hapi had his home. He took with him offerings of every kind to persuade the god to look kindly on the kingdom once more.

But when the chief priest reached the cave where Hapi lived, he found it was shut up, with iron bars across the door. Hapi was trapped, which was why the Nile could not rise.

The priest realized at once that it was another god, ram-headed Khnem, who had imprisoned Hapi. Khnem, too, was a river god, and some said that he was even more ancient than his rival, Hapi.

The priest knew exactly what to do. Dealing with difficult gods was part of his training. He took the offerings he had brought for Hapi and presented them to Khnem instead.

Needless to say, Khnem was delighted. He unlocked Hapi's cave and let the god go about his business once more.

That year, the waters of the Nile rose and flooded the land as usual. Where once there had been desert, crops flourished. The people smiled again, and the king rewarded his chief priest for his cleverness.

And even the gods forgot to quarrel.

THE LEOPARD
AND THE JACKAL

One day, Leopard and Jackal went out hunting. Leopard caught a frisky goat, but Jackal did even better and brought home a fine cow.

When the cow and the goat were safely tethered, Leopard and Jackal went to bed, but Leopard could not sleep. He was jealous of Jackal's cow. And when he went out in the night and found that the cow had given birth to a calf, he was even more annoyed. He stole the calf and put it with his goat.

In the morning, Jackal was not deceived for one moment.

"Only cows have calves," he said. "That is definitely my calf."

"Nonsense," said Leopard, "but don't just take my word for it. Let's go and ask Gazelle."

Now Gazelle was afraid of Leopard, so she said, "Calves used to come from cows, it's true, but I believe they can come from goats, too, these days."

When Jackal appealed to Hyena and Klipspringer, both were too afraid of Leopard to tell the truth.

Jackal was desperate. "Let's go and ask Baboon," he said.

But Baboon refused to answer. He just plucked at a large stone. The animals waited respectfully. Eventually, Leopard could bear it no longer.

"What on earth are you doing?" he asked.

"Why, I'm playing music from this stone," said Baboon. "Can't you see?"

"You can't get music from an ordinary stone," scoffed Leopard.

Baboon smiled. "Music used to come from instruments, it's true," he said, "but these days I believe it can come from ordinary stones, too."

Then the animals all around laughed.

"He's joking," they said. "Of course you can't get music from a stone. And you can't get a calf from a goat, either!"

Leopard knew when he was beaten – the calf was returned to Jackal.

The Hare Wants a Wife

Trickster Hare decided it was time to take a wife. But wives expect their husbands to work hard, clearing all the large trees and bushes from the land so that the wife can sow and reap.

Trickster Hare didn't want to work hard. His quick and clever brain had an idea. He took a large rope and set off to find Hippopotamus.

Hippopotamus was wallowing in the muddy river.

"You know, Hippopotamus," said Hare, "I believe I'm as strong as you. Take hold of the end of this rope, and, when you feel me pull it, pull yourself as hard as you can. I bet you can't pull me into the river."

Now Hippopotamus knew he could pull Hare with no trouble at all, but still, he agreed to the strange request.

Then Trickster Hare went to find Elephant. The giant creature was munching leaves at the edge of the forest.

"You know, Elephant," said Hare, "I believe I'm as strong as you. Take hold of the end of this rope, and, when you feel me pull it, pull yourself as hard as you can. I bet you can't pull me into the forest."

Now Elephant was puzzled by Hare's question. He knew he was much stronger than the smaller animal. But still, he agreed.

Then Trickster Hare gave a little tug on the rope and slipped quietly away.

Of course, as soon as Hippopotamus felt the tug on the rope, he pulled as hard as he could. And when Elephant felt that pull, he set his mighty shoulders and p-u-l-l-e-d.

Back and forth, back and forth, all day long the huge animals pulled that rope, until there wasn't a bush or a tree standing between the edge of the forest and the river. And clever old Hare, with so much fine land cleared, got just the wife he wanted!

THE VERY CLEVER WIFE

There was once a great chief who prided himself on his cleverness. Whenever there was a dispute between two of his people, he found a way to solve it.

One day, the chief met his match. He found a woman who was both beautiful and clever. The chief decided to make her his wife, but on one matter he was clear.

"I am the problem-solver in this household," he told her. "Don't ever try to interfere with my work. If you do, I will send you straight back to where you came from."

For a long while, the chief's wife was careful not to get involved in matters that were really the chief's concern, but one day she couldn't resist. The solution to a problem was so obvious that she couldn't help giving her own advice.

The chief was furious.

"I told you what I would do if this happened," he shouted. "Choose one thing from this house to take away with you and leave. I want you to be gone in the morning."

Now the chief and his wife were very well matched indeed. Neither of them wanted to part from the other. But the chief's pride had been wounded, and he refused to back down. That night, saddened by what had happened and urged on by his wife, he drank far more palm wine than was good for him and fell into a deep, deep sleep.

At once, his wife had him carried to her family home. When the chief woke in the morning, he demanded to know what on earth was going on.

"Ah," said his wife, "you said that I could take one thing away with me, and there is truly only one thing in our home that I would want to have with me always. It is you! So I brought you here."

Despite his throbbing head, the chief could not help but smile. With such a clever wife, who could blame him?

THE PARTY OF THE GREAT CHIEF

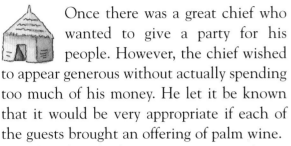 Once there was a great chief who wanted to give a party for his people. However, the chief wished to appear generous without actually spending too much of his money. He let it be known that it would be very appropriate if each of the guests brought an offering of palm wine.

The chief had a great container hewn from the trunk of a tree to contain the wine. On the appointed day, as each guest arrived, he or she would pour an offering into the container.

Everyone was very excited about the party, but one man was worried. He was a very poor farmer and he had absolutely no palm wine to take to the party. It wasn't until the day of the party itself that he had an idea. He filled his gourd with water instead of wine.

Well, everything happened just as the chief had planned. As the guests arrived, they poured their offerings into the big wooden container.

At last it was the turn of the poor man. Swiftly pouring in his gourdful of water, he reasoned that no one would be able to taste so little water in such a big vat of wine.

At last the time came for everyone to drink to the great chief. Cups were filled from the huge container and flattering words were said. Then everyone threw back their heads and drank.

At once there was a gasp of horror from the crowd and a bellow of fury from the chief. They were all drinking water!

You see, every one of the guests had had exactly the same idea as the poor man. In this case, it was the chief who learned a lesson. For a host who is not generous does not deserve to be called a host at all.

THE HIPPOPOTAMUS AND THE TORTOISE

Now there was a time when Hippo lived on land and was second only to Elephant in wealth and power. Every so often, Hippo gave a great feast and invited all his animal friends. But the strange thing was that although they knew Hippo well, none of these visitors knew his real name. Only Hippo's seven fat wives knew that.

One day, when he had summoned all the animals to a feast, Hippo made an important announcement. "More and more of you come each time," he said. "I've decided that in future only those of you who know my true name can stay. I'm afraid the rest of you will have to go home without enjoying my hospitality."

Well, the animals went home, but there was quite a lot of grumbling and muttering. Only Tortoise had the courage to speak up.

"Hippo!" he cried. "If, next time, I can tell you your true name, what will you do?"

"I will feel ashamed," said Hippo, "and I and my wives will leave the land and go to live in the water."

Next day, Tortoise hurried to a nearby waterhole and half-buried himself in the sand. When Hippo and his wives came by to drink, one of the wives hit her toe on Tortoise's hard shell.

"Oh, Isantim, my husband, I have hurt my foot!" she cried.

Of course, now Tortoise knew Hippo's true name. He scuttled off in delight.

The next feast came, and Tortoise had no hesitation in standing up. "Oh, Isantim," he shouted, "thank you for this delicious food!"

Then Hippo knew that his bluff had been called and, as he promised, he took his wives to live in the water. They are living there to this very day.

THE CROCODILE AND THE HEN

In the waters of the mighty Zaire River lived Crocodile, and she was always hungry. No creature in the river, or on the river, or beside the river was safe from her powerful jaws.

One day, plump Hen came down to the river to drink.

"Ha, ha!" said Crocodile. "Dinner!"

But when Crocodile thrust her snout out of the water and opened her huge mouth, Hen looked up without concern. "Good morning, sister," she said.

Crocodile shut her mouth with a *snap!* Somehow, she couldn't quite bring herself to eat someone who called her "sister". It didn't seem right.

Day after day, the same thing happened. Crocodile badly wanted to eat Hen. She wanted it more each time she saw the plump little bird. At last, Crocodile could bear it no longer. She decided to find out exactly what kind of kin Hen could possibly be.

Crocodile left the river and set out to find some answers. As the hot sun beat down, the first creature she met was Lizard, and Lizard was known to be pretty wise.

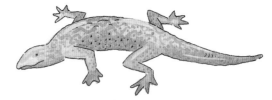

"Lizard," said Crocodile, "I've got a problem. As you know, I like to eat anything that moves, but when Hen comes to the river, she calls me "sister". I live in the water. She lives on land. I have scales. She has feathers. I have a nose. She has a beak. I have four legs. She has two legs and two wings. How can we possibly have anything in common, let alone be related?"

"Oh, Crocodile," smiled Lizard. "Don't you know that you don't have to look alike to be kin? Why, you and I and Hen and Turtle and Ostrich and lots of other creatures are all alike for one very important reason. Though we don't look the same, or act the same, or think the same, we all lay eggs. So that makes us sisters."

And that is why Crocodile never eats Hen.

THE OSTRICH AND THE GEMSBOK

When the world was young, Ostrich was black and white all over, with a striped neck and head and two long, slender horns. He looked magnificent.

Gemsbok, who was a dull brown all over, was jealous. One day, he challenged Ostrich to a race. "However, I am much faster than you," said Gemsbok, "so to make matters fairer, I will carry your heavy horns and wear your stripy scarf and hat.

Ostrich agreed and off they went. Now Ostrich should really have had the advantage, but Gemsbok was clever as well as fast. He made sure that he raced over every stony, rough piece of ground he knew. It was fine for Gemsbok's horny feet – he skipped and pranced over the rockiest terrain – but Ostrich had soft feet, used to running on the grassy plains. It was not long before he was hobbling and staggering, no match for the cunning Gemsbok.

So Gemsbok kept Ostrich's horns and hat and scarf and left the bird with a long, dull, brown neck with a small, naked head on top.

Clever Gemsbok was delighted with his new horns. He exercised hard and soon found that they were useful for fighting his enemies. He loved his handsome black and white face, too, when he glimpsed it reflected in the waterhole.

At first, Ostrich was very angry, but it wasn't long before he realized that life was much, much easier without the heavy horns he used to wear. He could run faster, and they didn't get in the way when he pecked at his food. And maybe Ostrich was pretty clever, too, for it occurred to him that if he made friends with Gemsbok, those horns could defend Ostrich, too.

Ostrich and Gemsbok are still often seen together. Maybe now we know why.

UNKULUNKULU AND THE PEOPLE OF EARTH

It was Unkulunkulu who, when the world was only a watery, wild place, took reeds from a swamp and made the first people. When he had finished, he gave them every good thing they would need – water, crops, meat, fish, fire and good health. The only thing he had not so far given the people was the ability to live for ever, but this he decided to do.

Unkulunkulu called Chameleon to him and pointed to the moon in the sky. "Tell the people," he said, "that they will waste away and die, as the moon dies every month, but that like the moon, they will always live and grow again."

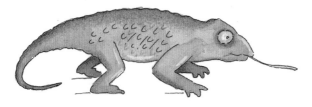

Chameleon set off with this important message. He knew that when the word of Unkulunkulu was spoken to the people, it would come to pass.

Now Chameleon was slow and steady, but he took so long to reach the people that Unkulunkulu became impatient and called for Hare. He gave him exactly the same message to take to the people.

Hare raced along. Of course, he reached the people of earth before Chameleon. But Hare was also careless. He didn't tell the people what Unkulunkulu had said. He told them what he thought he had said.

"Like the moon, you will live and grow," he announced, "but as the moon dies every month, you will waste away and die."

When the people heard this, they went away with drooping heads and deep sighs. There was nothing that Chameleon or even Unkulunkulu himself could do, for once his words have been spoken, they come to pass.

And that is why, to this day, the people of the earth have everything they need, except the one thing they long for – immortality.

OCEANIA

THE ANTEATER
AND THE TURTLE

Long ago in the Dreamtime, Anteater and Turtle were great friends. Anteater did not have any spines on her back, and Turtle did not have a shell on his back. They simply had no need for them.

One day, Anteater was hungry and needed to go out hunting for food. She asked her friend Turtle to look after her baby while she was gone.

"It'll be a pleasure," said Turtle. And he did look after the baby very well indeed, until he too began to be hungry. Turtle could not leave the baby to look for food. He tried to forget how hungry he was. But Anteater was gone a long, long time, so Turtle did what seemed the best thing. He ate Anteater's baby.

Of course, when Anteater came back, she asked, "Where's my baby?"

Turtle didn't say a word. He looked at the sky. He looked at the bush. He looked at his own claws. Anteater realized with horror what had happened.

Poor Anteater could hardly take in what had happened. In her fury and grief, she picked up a stone and hurled it at Turtle.

She threw stone after stone at her one-time friend, and some of them stuck in his back.

Turtle rushed off as quickly as he could and grabbed his spears. One by one, he threw them at Anteater. Some fell off, but most of them stuck in her back and stayed there.

Well, those spears are still in Anteater's back to this day, but they have become her spines. And the stones are still on Turtle's back and form his shell.

Neither Anteater nor Turtle has much to fear from enemies these days, but then, they do not have many friends either.

HOW THE KIWI
LOST HIS WINGS

 One day, Tanemahuta was walking in the cool of the forest when he noticed that some of his children, the trees, were not well. Their branches were drooping and their leaves were dying.

Then Tanemahuta knew that the trees would never recover if one of the birds who lived high in the treetops did not come down to live on the forest floor instead. And if the trees died, the birds would disappear, too.

Tanemahuta called up to the birds as they sang and fluttered overhead.

"Which one of you will come down," he said, "and save your brothers, the trees?"

But one by one the birds refused. They looked at the dark, cold earth below. They looked around at the sunlight that was shining on the leaves above.

"All of my family is here. I cannot leave them," chirruped one.

"I am busy building my nest. I can't stop now," twittered another.

Tanemahuta's heart was very heavy. Last of all, he asked the kiwi if he would be willing to come to live far below.

The kiwi looked around at the sunshine.

He saw his family and his nest. But he knew what he must do.

"I will come," he said.

"Do you understand what this means?" asked Tanemahuta. "Your legs will become thick and stocky, so that you can scratch at the earth and rotting logs. Your beautiful feathers will become dull and brown. You will no longer be able to fly, so you will never see the treetops or the other birds again.

"I understand," said the kiwi, "and I am willing to come."

Then Tanemahuta's heart was filled with joy, for he knew that the trees would be saved and the birds could live on in the forest.

"You may not be beautiful," he told the kiwi, "but because of your courage, you will become the best-loved bird in the land."

CAT AND MOUSE GO BOATING

 Once upon a time, Cat and Mouse were great friends. They lived in the rainforest together and were perfectly happy. Cat mainly ate small birds, and Mouse mostly enjoyed a kind of sweet potato called *taro*. But one day, Cat became restless.

"Mouse," said Cat, "I think we should leave the forest and find a village to live in. There will be lots of houses there, and you know how careless humans are. We'll find plenty of food lying about without us having to hunt for it. Our lives will be much easier."

"But," said Mouse, "we live on an island where there are no villages. How are we going to reach the mainland?"

"I've thought of that," said Cat. "We could hollow out a boat from a particularly big *taro*. What do you think of that?"

"I think I'd enjoy making that boat!" laughed Mouse. And so he did.

Cat and Mouse set sail a week or so later. Their boat was seaworthy, but it was heavy to paddle. Before long, Cat and Mouse were exhausted. They were very far from land.

Of course, they were getting hungry, too. One night, while Cat was sleeping, Mouse found himself looking longingly at the *taro* boat. Just a little nibble couldn't hurt…

But one little nibble turned into a lot of big nibbles, and before Mouse knew it, the boat began to leak. At once, Cat woke up.

"Mouse, I know exactly what you've been up to! When we reach land I'm going to eat you!" he cried, before both Mouse and Cat were thrown into the sea and had to swim for it.

Once on shore, Cat looked hungrily at Mouse, but Mouse urged him to wait. "I'm very dirty and salty," he said. "Let me just give myself a wash before you eat me. Here's a little hole where I can do it."

Mouse disappeared … and did not reappear. He dug a little tunnel and escaped. So you can understand, can't you, why Cat and Mouse are no longer such great friends?

THE BIRDS WHO WOULD BE BRIGHT

Long ago two birds lived in the rainforest. One was completely black. The other was white underneath and green on top. It was hard to see either of them among the leaves and branches of the forest.

Seeing more brightly feathered birds flashing through the trees, the green and white bird decided to spruce himself up. He found a special red leaf. Then he dug a small hole in the ground, filled it with water and squeezed the leaf into it. The water in the tiny pool turned bright red.

Off went the green and white bird to have a good wash before dyeing his feathers. While he was gone, the black bird flew down to see what his friend had been doing. He was so curious that he dipped his head right into the red water.

When the green and white bird came back, he ran towards the waterhole and jumped, expecting to land with a splash right in the middle of the dye. But there wasn't much of a splash at all, as most of the dye seemed to have mysteriously disappeared. Only a few drops splashed the bird's white tummy.

It was an improvement, but it wasn't at all what the green and white bird had had in mind. He sat down on his usual branch so that his feathers could dry. He began to wonder what had happened to the rest of the dye.

Just then, a careless kind of whistling could be heard on a branch above. The green, white and (very slightly) red bird looked up. There sat a black bird with a red head and neck – who looked somehow suspiciously familiar!

I'm afraid that those birds are no longer friends. The green and white and (very slightly) red bird was so cross that he went to live deep in the rainforest. He is still pretty hard to find. As for the black bird with the red head, he is so proud of himself that he hops around villages and places where there are people, making sure *everyone* sees him!

THE FLOWERS OF TEARS

Love is a very powerful thing, as this story shows. It tells of a beautiful young girl, the daughter of a great chief. Her name was Adi Perena.

Now, the daughter of a chief should marry a powerful man, someone who can bring even more prestige to her father, but Adi Perena fell in love with someone quite unsuitable.

Taitusi was very poor. True, he was good and kind and handsome, but he was not the kind of husband a chief wants for his beloved daughter.

Adi Perena could not hide her feelings. Before long, even her father found out why her eyes sparkled and her skin glowed. He decided to do something about it. To her horror, Adi Perena found that she was to marry Tuki Kuto, a very old man.

The desperate girl could not bear the thought of marrying anyone but her beloved Taitusi. She walked alone along the beach and decided there was only one thing to do.

The next morning, Adi Perena left her father's house at dawn, before anyone else was awake.

As the sun rose in the sky, Adi Perena climbed through the foothills and up the forested slopes of the high mountains of her homeland. Higher and higher she climbed, until she came to a lake in the midst of the mountains. Here, exhausted, she could go no further. She lay down in the leafy rainforest and fell fast asleep.

So distressed was Adi Perena that she wept even in her sleep. As her tears fell, they turned into flowers – beautiful blossoms with red petals outside and white within. This is the flower that is known as Tagimoucia, or "sleeping tears". It can still be found in Fiji, but nowhere else in the world.

When Adi Perena's father found her at last, amid the beautiful flowers she had created, his heart softened, and he allowed her to marry Taitusi after all.

THE SEVEN HEADS OF STONE

 The Pacific Ocean has thousands of islands. There are large ones with cities and airports. There are tiny ones with room for only one small turtle. But just because there are thousands of them doesn't mean they are close together. The Pacific Ocean is huge, and some islands are a very, very long way from the nearest land.

The most isolated inhabited island of all is called Easter Island.

Many years ago, the Polynesian lord Hotu Matu'a was looking for a land of his own. Like many of his people, Hotu Matu'a had many tattoos on his face and body. One day, when his tattooist came to add to these patterns, Hotu Matu'a talked about his hopes for a new land across the sea.

"Sir, it is strange that you should say so," said the tattooist, whose name was Haumaka. "Last night I dreamed of just such a land. It was far, far away, but it had long, long beaches of clean, white sand."

These words gave Hotu Matu'a the nudge he needed. He prepared a special expedition to search for Haumaka's dreamland. Seven hand-picked men set off in a boat.

But as the weeks passed, Hotu Matu'a became impatient. With his wife and family and many of his followers, the lord set out after the expedition.

At long last, Hotu Matu'a reached land, where he found another boat pulled up on the shore. Just as the earlier expedition came back from exploring the island, Hotu Matu'a's wife gave birth to a son on the sandy beach of the new land.

Hotu Matu'a was sure this was a sign. He settled there with all his people.

Today, the most striking features of Easter Island are seven stone heads, looking out to sea. Some say that these are the statues of the seven explorers who first found the island – but no one really knows.

The Mutiny on the Bounty

In the vast Pacific Ocean there are many islands. Hundreds of years ago, when navigation was much more difficult than it is today, it could be very difficult to find one small island among many. On one occasion, that is exactly what the sailors wanted!

In 1787, a ship called *HMS Bounty* set sail from England. The plan was to sail to Tahiti, take on board hundreds of breadfruit plants, and then sail on to the Caribbean, where the breadfruit would be planted to feed the slaves who were working there.

All went more or less according to plan until the ship reached Tahiti. It took many months to harvest the breadfruit, and during that time the sailors became used to their life on shore. They were also dazzled by the Tahitian women, who are renowned throughout the world for their beauty.

When the time came for the *Bounty* to set sail, no one was very eager to go. Some say that the captain, William Bligh, was a harsh man. Others think that the soft life on Tahiti was the cause. Whatever it might have been, on 28th April 1789, twelve members of the crew, led by Master's Mate Fletcher Christian, mutinied. They set Bligh and loyal crew members adrift in an open boat and sailed back to Tahiti.

Christian knew that he needed to find somewhere to hide. The punishment for mutiny was death. After collecting the women they had grown fond of on Tahiti, the group sailed on, looking for an island that would be hard to find.

Pitcairn Island was perfect. It had no natural port for other ships to dock in, and better still, it was in the wrong position by two hundred miles on the maps that other ships would be using! The mutineers struggled ashore and sank the *Bounty*.

Although Bligh reached safety, the mutineers were not discovered until only one was still alive. Nevertheless, their descendants live on Pitcairn Island to this day.

THE GREAT STORM

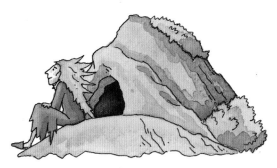

There was once a boy called Maui who made a kite from barkcloth and bamboo. He longed to fly it, but the day was still and warm. Maui went off to the Cave-of-the-Winds for help.

The Keeper-of-the-Winds, who was an old woman, was sitting outside. When she heard what Maui needed, she agreed to his request. Taking a small gourd out of the cave, she said some magic words and opened it very slightly. Out came a gentle breeze, then another one, until there was just the right amount of movement in the air for Maui to fly his kite.

The boy had a wonderful time. He screamed with delight as he ran along the beach, his kite soaring high above him.

At last Keeper-of-the-Winds said that it was time for the winds to return to the cave. Sadly, Maui agreed.

The next day, Maui wanted to fly his kite again, but he had grown ambitious. "I want a really big wind," he said. "I want my kite to fly higher than any kite has ever flown!"

"Hush!" said the Keeper-of-the-Winds. "The mighty winds are too strong for you."

But it was too late. The winds inside the cave had heard the boy call to them. They came rushing out, storming over the island and knocking down palm trees, huts and anything else that stood in their way. The sky became dark, and the sea lashed the land. Maui clung to the Keeper-of-the-Winds in fright as she desperately tried to call the mighty winds back into their cave.

All night long the Keeper-of-the-Winds worked. Slowly the great winds came home, until the island was still. But everywhere there were terrible scenes as people looked for loved ones or tried to rebuild their homes. It was a long time before anyone would speak to Maui, and the boy learned that the forces of nature are too powerful to be treated as a game.

THE TURTLE AND THE SHARK

In the village of Vaitogi there lived an old woman who had a very beautiful daughter. The woman worried a good deal about the girl, especially when she stayed out late with her friends.

"Late at night is when the evil spirits are about," she warned her daughter. "What if you are caught by one?"

But the girl simply laughed. She was sure that wouldn't happen to *her*. In fact, she began staying out later and later. Back at home, her mother paced the floor, eaten up with fear for her daughter.

One night, when the girl returned, almost at dawn, she was met by other people from the village and told that her mother had died a few hours before.

"She was worn out with worry about *you*, you selfish girl," said one villager, brushing away her own tears.

The daughter was overcome by grief. She went down to the seashore in the moonlight and prayed to the gods for her mother to be given back to her. And the gods, moved by her sorrow, sent back her mother in the form of a turtle.

This helped the girl a great deal. She spent as much time with the turtle as she could, but, of course, the turtle lived in the sea and always had to return there. Then the girl was once more heart-broken. She longed to be with her mother all the time.

So the girl prayed to the gods again and asked that she be turned into a sea creature too, so that she and her mother need never be parted. The gods once more looked kindly on her, and turned her into a shark.

To this day, you will still see the turtle and the shark together near the shores of Vaitogi, for the mother and her daughter have never been parted again.